Family Tree

Family
Tree

Katherine Ayres

A Yearling Book

Published by
Bantam Doubleday Dell Books for Young Readers
a division of
Bantam Doubleday Dell Publishing Group, Inc.
1540 Broadway
New York, New York 10036

Visit us on the Web! www.bdd.com

Educators and librarians, visit the BDD Teacher's Resource Center at www.bdd.com/teachers

ISBN: 0-440-41193-9

Reprinted by arrangement with Delacorte Press

Printed in the United States of America

December 1997

10 9 8 7 6 5

OPM

For my parents, Ray and Betty Kent

Prologue

I sat in the backseat of the bus and looked out. The sun was already high, and the trees wore a film of red-brown dust. Why was the first day of school always so hot? This was Ohio, after all, not Texas or Alabama.

We'd always have a day or two of crisp weather late in August, to warn us that summer was almost over. Then, when we were going to be cooped up all day and wouldn't mind cool, or even rain, we'd get a blistering heat wave. No fair.

I pushed my hair off my neck and remembered back. Seemed like every year from kindergarten on, the first day of school had been blazing. Not that I really remembered the weather from that long ago. When I'd gone to kindergarten, I'd had so much else to learn, I'd probably missed the first snowstorm.

I was a real strange kid back then. I didn't even know I was a girl for the first half of my life. I didn't think I was a boy or anything; I just didn't know the difference. I was a little person. Papa was a big person. That's what I knew. So school was a shock.

As the bus pulled up the long driveway to Pine View Elementary, I shook off the remembering. Hot or not, it was the first day of a new school year, and I wanted to be ready for it. I wanted to get off to a good start. It wouldn't do for the new teacher to catch me daydreaming. Especially not this new teacher.

Chapter 1

"Tyler. Tyler Stoudt."

Ms. Custer said my name twice. I sat up straight and raised my hand.

Ms. Martha Custer was the strictest teacher in the whole school. We'd heard about her since we were just babies in kindergarten. Now, in sixth grade, we were the oldest. We'd gotten the toughest teacher of all.

She stepped close to my desk. "Interesting name. Haven't run across another girl named Tyler in thirty years of teaching."

"Yes, ma'am," I said. "It's a family name." I always said that when people asked. It kept them from scowling at me and my odd name.

"Your father's family or your mother's?" she asked.

I frowned. Most people just let it go as a family name. Ms. Custer didn't let it go. Ms. Custer wasn't most people. Last year's sixth-graders were right. First day of school, and already we had a hard year coming.

"Mother's family," I answered. "Tyler was my mother's last name before she married Papa."

I didn't tell the rest of the story. How Mama had been killed in that terrible car wreck weeks and weeks before I was supposed to be born. Or how the doctors had worked hard to save me. Or how Papa had wanted to name me after my mother but couldn't make his mouth say the name *Sarah* day after day. So he picked her last name, Tyler, for me.

That name got me noticed right off—like having green hair or blue fingernails. Sometimes for good and sometimes not. Most days I was proud to be named after my mother. Let people like Sissy Norman giggle. I'd rather be a Tyler than a Sissy any day.

"Distinguished," Ms. Custer said. "One of our presidents was named Tyler. I'll expect you to live up to that name, young lady."

"Yes, ma'am." I nodded to her and watched,

letting my breath out slowly, while she went to stand next to Casey Powell.

She bent over and talked to him like she'd talked to me. I figured it must be her way of getting to know us.

I went back to work, writing my name in my new books and enjoying that first-day-of-school smell—fresh ink from the workbooks, new pencils sharpened for the first time. When I finished, I flipped open my notepad and wrote down the word the teacher had used about my name. *Distinguished*.

Teachers always told us to look up words we didn't know so we could build our vocabularies. Most kids just waited till they got home and asked their parents.

I always had to look them up. I couldn't ask Papa what English words meant. Sure, he had gone to school, but I knew more words than he did. Or I would have, except for the notepad. I'd take the new words home and we'd look them up together after supper. Every time I learned a hard one, he learned it, too. It was a game we played, Papa and I.

"Ladies and gentlemen," Ms. Custer said. She stood next to her desk in the front of the room. "Have you finished putting your names in your books? Excellent. Please put covers on those books tonight. I won't have uncovered books in my class. Understood? Excellent.

"Now, class, clear your desks and sit up straight. Slouching is not conducive to thinking." Ms. Custer gave us a minute to follow her orders.

I pulled my shoulders up and wondered what *conducive* meant, but I wasn't about to ask at that very moment. The teacher had an I-mean-business look in her eye. I couldn't write it in my notepad either, since she wanted empty desks. I sat up as tall as I could and waited. I didn't have to wait long.

"I shall be very clear with you, ladies and gentlemen. My expectations this year are high. I don't want slouching in your posture or your work habits. I value honesty, curiosity, and hard work. I expect that of myself, and I expect that of each of you. In addition, I require respect in my classroom. I will respect you. You will respect me. And you will respect each other. That's it. Those are the rules. Live with them and you will succeed. Break them and you will not. Questions?"

It got so quiet I could hear a fly buzzing in the front window by the blackboard. I traded looks with Casey Powell. I rolled my eyes. He scowled. Ms. Custer sounded tough, all right. She wasn't

Ms. Custer smiled. "That's right. Family trees. As we move around the world in our studies, you'll share information on the countries your families came from. We'll read books from those cultures as well. And in science we'll study real trees. How forests grow and change."

I smiled. I'd do fine in the science part, because I'd practically grown up in the woods. But the family part would take some work. I bent over my desk and wrote carefully. *Sarah Tyler. Jakob Stoudt.* I filled in their birthdates in pencil because I needed to check with Papa to be sure of the years. Then I wrote *English* beside Mama's name and *Deutsch* beside Papa's.

Ms. Custer walked around the room looking over our papers. "Oh yes," she said, nodding and smiling. "We'll have a good year together, I can tell already. Several of your parents came from other countries."

She stopped at my desk and pointed to Papa's name. She spoke low and private. "*Deutsch.* Is that how he spells it, or is it *Dutch*?"

"*Deutsch,*" I whispered.

"German, then," she said. "Your father comes from Germany."

I knew that, but I was used to Papa's saying *Deutsch.* I wrote *German* underneath the word

Deutsch while she covered the ground between my desk and the front of the room.

Her voice rolled on with the assignment, and all around me kids scribbled. "Now, as you did with your own name, draw a V above each of your parents' names and fill in the names and birthdates of your grandparents. Then the great-grandparents. Both sides."

She flipped on the overhead projector and showed us her own family tree. Names and dates covered three whole pages in ever smaller branches. Grandparents, aunts, uncles, and more cousins than you'd believe. The farther I looked from Ms. Custer's own name, the more her family tree looked like a gigantic web, spun by a monster spider. I felt myself pulled into that web, and the strands began to squeeze at me.

"Your assignment for the rest of the week is to fill in the chart, as far back as you can. Those of you with parents and grandparents born in America, go back in the generations to find the people who first came here and where they came from. Any questions?"

Hands waved in the air around me as kids asked where to put great-grandparents and what to do if you had a stepfather. My fingers closed up tight on my pen, and sweat gathered in the palm of my hand.

What a terrible start. I had the toughest teacher in three counties. A woman who called sixth-graders "ladies and gentlemen." And she planned to spend the entire year teaching us about the world by using family trees. Kids on both sides of me were asking for extra sheets of paper.

From what I could see, this dumb family tree was the most important assignment we'd get all year. Everything else depended on it—reading, science, social studies, everything! A whole year's work!

I glared at the mostly white page in front of me and wished.

But no matter how hard I wished, I'd never have more than three names on my paper.

I'd have to flunk the sixth grade.

Chapter 2

"So how was school, *liebchen*? Like your new teacher?"

Papa stood at his workbench in the barn with a heavy plane in his hands. Bits of sawdust clung to his blue workshirt and even his shaggy brown hair and beard.

I picked up a fresh curl of pine wood and stuck it under my nose. I loved the smells in Papa's wood shop, and it felt cool here, a relief from the hot, stuffy school building. "My teacher's okay, Papa." I tried to sound like I meant it.

"She was mean like you worried about?" he asked.

"Strict," I said. "Not mean yet." But she would be. She'd be especially mean to me when I slouched. When I didn't have a family tree to hand in on Monday.

Papa dusted wood shavings off his hands and pulled me into a hug. "Sixth grade already. You've grown so big I can hardly believe it."

I wasn't big, not compared to Papa, who had wide shoulders and strong arms and towered over me like a big old pine tree. I was mostly average for my age. Plain brown eyes, plain brown hair, not tall, but not short either. I wasn't particularly ugly, but I sure wasn't a magazine beauty. Just an ordinary girl.

"What's her name, this strict teacher?" Papa asked.

"Ms. Custer."

"Custard? Like pudding?"

Papa was joking to cheer me up, but it didn't work. "No. Just plain Custer."

"She won't be another flower teacher, will she?" he asked. He took my chin in his hand and looked down into my face.

I had to laugh, even at the thought.

I shook my head. "Too old, Papa. Way too old for you."

"*Ach.* Too bad," he said with a grin. He turned back to the boards on his workbench and felt for rough spots.

I watched his strong hands lift the plane and run it along the pine, raising curls of wood. I remembered the flower teacher.

Kindergarten. I spoke a mixture of English and Deutsch and I hadn't seen many children or women before, not close up. So when I got to know my teacher, when I had a chance to soak up her kindness and warmth, I'd wanted her for my mama. By then I knew the rest of the kids had a mama, and I pestered Papa about why I didn't.

The flower teacher. Her name was Ms. Holden, and she smelled like flowers. Now I know she used perfume, but then I thought she lived in a meadow where wildflowers grew. I liked every single thing about her, from her sweet smell to the way she welcomed us with a soft touch and a cheery smile every morning. I'd been trying to think of a way for her to meet Papa when Casey Powell helped me out.

Of course, Casey hadn't known he was helping. He got into a fight with an older boy on his bus, a second-grader. He bit the boy and left a whole set of teeth marks. Ms. Holden called in Casey's parents for a meeting.

I wasn't the kind of girl to start a fight. I hardly knew what to do around all those kids. I mostly watched them like I watched the blue jays and the cardinals in our backyard. But if I got into trouble, the flower teacher would have to call Papa. So I took things. Lunch boxes. School papers. I ripped a few paintings and hid Sissy Norman's favorite sweater behind the big blocks.

Sure enough, Ms. Holden had called Papa.

I never knew what they said at the meeting. All I remember is asking Papa, "Do you like her? Do you like the flower teacher? Won't she make a good mama?"

Papa had looked at me funny then, and he called the teacher on the telephone. I remember that especially, because he didn't use the phone very often. The next day Ms. Holden took me aside and said how nice I made her feel, wanting her for my mama, but how she was my teacher instead and my friend.

Kindergarten. A long time ago. Over the years, I'd had good luck in school. Once my teachers found out I didn't have a mama, they always took special care of me. That wouldn't happen this year, though. Ms. Custer wouldn't find out how much I loved books, or all the things I knew about birds and animals. She'd write me down in her grade book as a slouching, lazy kid who didn't get her work done.

I sighed as I watched Papa measure his boards

15

and cut them with his saw. He was making a table, and the boards were the top.

I never got tired of watching his hands. It was a kind of miracle, the way he took plain, flat lumber and turned it into beautiful tables or desks or cupboards. He didn't use power tools, either, just the strength in his own hands and the sharp saws and planes and drills he hung so carefully above the workbench.

I picked up my curl of pine and carried it with me to the house, breathing in the fresh smell. I grew up on the smell of wood, of glue and varnish. No wonder I'd loved the flower teacher.

I put away my new books and changed into an old pair of shorts. I checked the garden for weeds and picked a basketful of beans and two tomatoes. I found ripe sweet corn, too, so I pulled off a few ears. With Sunday's ham still sitting in the refrigerator, we'd have a fine supper.

I didn't mind snapping beans or shucking corn. I was actually proud—I could cook like a grown-up. I'd surprise my friends with special homemade pie when we got to the end of the year and had our school graduation picnic. If I got to graduate at the end of the year, that is. If I didn't flunk Ms. Custer's class and have to spend the rest of my life in sixth grade.

After supper, Papa pulled down the dictionary from the shelf. "New words today?" he asked.

I nodded. *"Distinguished,"* I told him. "My teacher says Tyler is a distinguished name."

"What you think it means?" he asked.

"I've heard it before. But I don't get it. When they call somebody distinguished, he's old and famous. I'm not either one."

"*Ja,* we'll look it up. *D-I-S?*"

"That's right, Papa."

He ran his finger up and down the page, and then he frowned. "Lots of meanings, Tyler. You pick one that fits." He passed me the heavy book.

He was right. Three inches of meanings for *distinguished.* Two caught my eye. One meant famous. Important. The other meant separated out. Different. Much as I hoped for the first meaning, a sinking feeling in my belly told me the second was more likely with Ms. Custer. I told both to Papa and closed the dictionary.

I guess my worry stuck out on my face, because Papa asked, "*Liebchen,* what's wrong? What happened at school?"

So I told him about Ms. Custer's plan to study the world through the families of kids in our class.

"Sounds interesting," he said. "You got kids with families from China and Africa, right?"

"Yes, Papa. But everybody's family matters." I reached over for my notebook and pulled out that terrible piece of white paper. "She wants us to make a family tree."

"Family tree?" He shook his head. "What? You need sticks and glue? Leaves? We got that."

I laughed. "Papa, you're always mixing things up. I don't need to make a real tree."

"What, then? Tree families. Like the different spruces or the kinds of walnut trees? That's it?"

I shook my head. If only Ms. Custer wanted tree families from us. That would be easy for me.

"No, Papa. Not spruces or walnuts. I need parents and grandparents. Aunts and uncles." I held the paper in front of him and showed him what I'd written so far. I pointed to the blank space above his name and Mama's. "I need to know about everybody, Papa. I need to fill up all the branches in my family tree."

A cold look came into his eyes. This always happened when I asked the wrong question. When I asked any question that went back to the times before he and Mama had come here to Ohio to live. As much as I wanted to know things, I'd mostly stopped asking. Papa would always shake his head and say, "Our family doesn't want to know us, Tyler. Better we forget about them." Why had I thought this time might be different?

He took my paper in his hands and studied it, shaking his head from side to side. Then, in one quick motion, he tore the paper in half.

I stared at the ripped paper in Papa's hands, the hands that once had carried a nest of baby mice far into the woods so they'd stay out of his shop. I'd never seen his hands shake so hard.

"I'll call the school," Papa said, his voice a low growl. "I'll call tomorrow morning."

"No, Papa. Please. My teacher's strict. I'll get in trouble."

"I'll write to the teacher, then," he said. "I'll write so you don't have to do this—this thing." He spat out the word *thing* like it burned his mouth, and he jabbed at the torn paper with his finger.

"Please, Papa. Just tell me their names. I don't need more than names. Everybody has to have a family tree."

"*Ja.* Everybody has a tree, *liebchen.*" His hands took mine and squeezed them gently. "But you, poor little Tyler, your family tree was chop down. Chop down and burnt up."

He shoved his chair back from the table and turned away, but not before I saw a shine of tears in his eyes.

My eyes filled then, but not with sadness. Ms. Custer was the meanest teacher in the whole world. She'd made me do the thing I hated most. She'd made me hurt Papa. So I hated her, too.

Chapter 3

By Friday I'd decided to lie about my family tree. I'd use Papa's name, and Mama's, and I'd make up a bunch of relatives. Aunts, uncles, cousins, and grandparents. Then I'd find some English and German names for my made-up relatives. How hard could that be?

My conscience itched. I shushed it.

Lying was a sin, but Papa wasn't too big on sins. He didn't say this was right and that was wrong. Mostly he asked what I thought. He talked about choices. What might happen if I did this thing instead of that thing.

I thought it out and decided that hurting Papa was a sin, too, right up there with disobeying one of the Ten Commandments. So I picked the sin that would cause the least trouble. Ms. Custer might not understand, but God would. Besides, if I was careful, Ms. Custer would never suspect.

At least I was luckier than some kids in my class. I knew which countries Mama and Papa came from. I just needed to know when they'd crossed the ocean. I waited until after supper to ask Papa. First I told him about science class, how we had to collect leaves and bark and wood from all sorts of trees.

"You will get an A on that, Tyler," he said. "You know every tree that grows in Ohio. You want wood from the shop?"

"Sure, Papa. Some for Casey, too. They cut down all the trees when they built his house, so I told him he could collect here. Okay?"

"Sure. We got enough trees for the whole class. You want to bring them all, maybe?"

"Maybe," I said. I was sure stinky old Ms. Custer would have liked to come out here. Bring everybody to our woods and study which trees grew where. Which ones liked sunlight and which preferred shade.

But when it came to Ms. Custer and trees of any kind, my temper still boiled.

The thought of her reminded me of the questions I needed to ask Papa. I swallowed hard and took a deep breath. If I could find the right way to ask this, he wouldn't get that cold look back in his eyes.

"Papa," I began. "Papa, when did you sail across the ocean? What year did you and Mama come to America?"

He looked at me and shook his head. "Ocean? I never sailed any ocean."

"So you took a plane, then. But when did you come? When did you come from Germany and Mama come from England?"

"Germany? England? Tyler, you don't make sense. You know your mama and I come here to Ohio from Pennsylvania."

"Yes. But before that. Before Pennsylvania. You came from Germany. She came from England."

"No. I come from Pennsylvania. Just Pennsylvania. Your mama never was in England. She come from Massachusetts." He stopped and paused for a minute, then continued. "South Egremont, Massachusetts."

His words mixed around in my head. "But she was English, Papa. You always say Mama was English."

Papa sighed, and his eyes grew cold, but helpless, too, this time. He knew why I was asking these questions.

"*Ja,* she was English. She talked English. But not from over the ocean."

"And you're Deutsch. You speak Deutsch. My teacher says that's German. So you're German."

"*Ja.* Deutsch." He stopped and looked at his hands, turning them over and studying them as though the words he needed to say were written there, in the creases and calluses.

"I was Deutsch," he continued, his voice soft. "But not German Deutsch. Not since a long time. Two hundred years. I was . . . I was Pennsylvania Deutsch. Plain. What the English call Amish."

I stared at him. My head was spinning so fast, I knew I'd fall if I tried to stand up.

Amish!

Eleven years old and what little I did know about my family was untrue. I had gotten it all mixed up—and my father had wanted it that way. Mama hadn't come from England; she was just an ordinary American. And Papa, with his strong German accent, Papa'd lived his whole life in Pennsylvania and Ohio.

He was Amish! One of those people with buggies and funny clothes.

"Tyler. Tyler."

His voice filtered through to me like it came

from far away. "This family tree thing again, yes? I knew I should have called that teacher."

I stared at him.

How had I missed the clues?

The longish haircut. The beard. Dark pants and shirt. Plain, he called it. Shoot, I'd heard that word enough times in my life. Plain as opposed to modern or fancy. Plain was good. Modern or fancy was bad.

"We need a long talk, you and me. You stay here on the sofa while I make some tea," Papa told me.

I sat back among the sofa cushions and twisted a strand of fringe between my fingers. I hoped Papa would take a while to make the tea. I needed time.

Amish!

My own father was Pennsylvania Dutch.

I squeezed my eyes tightly shut and tried to imagine him as a farm boy wearing one of those big black hats. The Amish were funny. Strange and old-fashioned.

But if that black hat didn't fit my image of Papa, the words sure did. At least the old-fashioned part. And, hard as it was to admit, Papa had ways about him that were funny. Not to me,

25

of course. But he was careful with outsiders. Suspicious of new ideas. Didn't talk much. And strange? Wasn't it strange for a parent to keep his whole life a secret from his daughter?

I swallowed past the lump in my throat. Amish. Funny. Old-fashioned. Strange.

I rolled those words over in my mind. If I stepped back and looked at Papa as an outsider might, Papa was all those things.

Then another thought hit. It hit hard and fast, like a punch in the stomach. If Papa was Amish, what about me?

Sure, I'd grown up different from the other kids. But now that I knew Papa was Amish, things began to make sense. For the first six years of my life I'd lived his childhood, the simple childhood of a plain Amish boy. I'd learned to fill the woodbox every morning and plant my own seeds in the garden each spring. I'd helped Papa catch fish for supper. And when the fish were biting, I'd cleaned my own catch and tossed it in cornmeal so Papa could fry it up, brown and crispy.

I'd sure had some catching up to do when I hit school. And I'd done okay, mostly. Kids and teachers liked me. At least I thought so.

But still I wondered. I ran my fingers through my hair, light brown and thick but chopped off short because Papa didn't know about braids or ponytails. "I'm good with wood, not with hair," he always said.

I stood up and headed for the old-fashioned mirror in the hall. I squinted at myself in the cloudy glass. Stared at the squarish face, the ruddy cheeks, the plain haircut. Shoot! How could I not have noticed? Put a wide, flat-brimmed hat on my head and I'd be a miniature version of Papa.

So what did that mean? I wondered as I stumbled back to the sofa.

Was I Amish, too?

Was I old-fashioned?

Strange?

Chapter 4

When Papa came back, he sat next to me and took one of my hands in his. "You're growing up, daughter," he said. "Eleven. Almost a dozen years. I'd thought to wait until you were older, but maybe you're old enough to understand."

"I'll try," I said.

He poured us each a cup of tea. It was a warm September evening, but I liked the feel of that hot cup in my hand.

"Where to begin? I'll tell what I can." He sat back and looked into his cup. A fortune-teller looks at tea leaves to read the future. My papa stared into that cup at the past.

"I was raised on a farm in Lancaster County.

Amish. I grew up like most plain boys. Helped my father on the farm. Played with my brothers—"

Brothers! My uncles! "How many brothers?" I interrupted.

He shook his head. "Later," he said. "I will tell what I can. In my own way."

I nodded, impatient for him to continue.

"I was an ordinary boy. Went to school with the English until I turn sixteen and they let me quit. Spent three years in the eighth grade. High school was too worldly. We had to flunk until they let us out. After, I learned to make furniture with one of the old men. It was good. I had the feel of the wood in my fingers."

Papa held out his hands palms up and looked at them. He wasn't bragging. He made it sound like his hands deserved all the credit for his skill. Like it was a gift he had received.

I looked around the room and saw all the places he used those hands—the rich, hand-rubbed finish on the cherry table in front of the sofa; the windows he'd taken apart and rebuilt so they wouldn't stick; the mantel over the fireplace, cut from a single wide board.

"Soon I made chairs and tables on my own," he explained. "So I built a shop on a piece of my father's land where the crops don't grow good. I

29

saved money. The English liked my furniture. They paid good prices. My father gave me another little piece of land next to my shop, where I could build a house. When I had the money for the house, I could start looking for a wife."

"Mama," I whispered. "You found Mama."

"No. Sarah found me."

Papa quit talking for a while.

I closed my eyes and tried to see it all as it had happened.

Then Papa took a deep breath and spoke again. "Your mama found me. She was not a woman I could take for a wife. She was English—American. She grew up with cars and lights. Every modern and fancy thing."

"How did she find you, Papa?" The knots in my stomach began to untangle. This was a story as good as any in the library books I loved. And at long last, Papa was telling me about his early life. I watched his eyes for signs of hurt, but instead he had a soft look. A remembering look.

He rubbed his hand on the knee of his pants. "You know that she wrote books, your mama. Wrote books and stories about people who choose a different way. She wrote about Shakers, who lived a long time ago. She visited Mormons and found a woman who told about growing up in a family with three wives."

"So she came to write a story about the Amish?"

"*Ja.* She wanted to make a book about a plain wedding. She come to Lancaster and spoke to people. My sister Dorcas was just promised to marry. Sarah asked to meet Dorcas and talk to her. Father first read the other books she wrote. He liked them. He and Mother told Dorcas she could talk to this English woman. Soon your mama spent lots of days in our house. She talked to everybody in the family. She put us all in the book."

"And you fell in love with her?" I knew better than to interrupt, but the story was so beautiful, I had to know it all.

"Not right away," Papa said. He smiled then. "Oh, I liked her, all right. She was very pretty, your mama. But she was English. Not for me.

"She came back to see us when her book was printed. Mother and Father liked the story, and we all read what she wrote. That's when I come to love your mama." He stopped and sighed, like it was hard to make the words come. Or maybe he was just remembering again. I didn't say anything, just waited.

"*Ja,* I fell in love with my Sarah when I read her book. She understood us. She told our life with truth and with . . . respect, I guess. She wanted to write another story. About me. About a man who worked with wood in the old ways. And that was it. The more we talked, the more we liked each other. After knowing Sarah, I could not imagine any other woman as my wife."

"And so you built your house and got married?" I was so wrapped up in the story, I made myself ignore the sad look that had crept into his eyes. I wanted a happy ending.

"No, Tyler. I did not build us a house. I knew better. I married your mother. Then we left."

"You left your family? But why? Why did you move away?"

"I was shunt."

"Shunt? I don't know that word." I stood up and reached for the dictionary, but Papa pulled me back.

"I said it wrong, Tyler. Shun-ned. I was shunned. *Verboten!*"

Hurt showed in his face now. Pain. I shivered from the look in his eyes and from that terrible word. *Verboten.* Forbidden.

Verboten! He'd shouted it when I was a baby, to keep my small fingers from poking into electrical sockets. He'd used it to warn me that the wood-stove was hot. It was the word for harmful things, for risks, for dangers. How could a *person* be *verboten*? A person strong and good like my papa?

He held his head in his hands and rested his elbows on his knees. At last I heard a long sigh.

"Your mother found me," he whispered. "We fell in love. So I married into the English."

He sighed again and raised his head to look at me. "They're a hard people, the Amish," he said. "The day I married my Sarah was for them the day I died."

I was watching Papa's face as he told his story. Now he bowed his head and looked away. Something about the way he turned his face aside told me to keep quiet.

It was hard. *I'm sorry,* I wanted to shout. *I'm sorry I brought this up. Sorry I cracked open the secret place where you hide all your sadness.*

I felt sorry about that and more. Sorry Papa'd had to leave behind his whole life to marry the woman he loved. Sorry he'd lost her in such a horrible accident. Poor Papa—he'd been left completely alone in the world with only me, a tiny baby.

But to tell the truth, I felt sorry for myself, too.

What had I ever done to deserve this? I hadn't broken any rules or stepped outside any lines.

Just like Papa, I had a family I couldn't love. Grandparents and aunts and uncles and cousins who wouldn't speak to me or to Papa.

At last I understood Papa's years of silence about his family. I felt hurt and left out and madder than a whole nest of yellow jackets.

Who gave those people the right to decide that Papa and I were *verboten*?

Chapter 5

Casey Powell arrived the next morning after breakfast, and I was so glad to see him I almost hugged him. I knew better, of course. Hugging would make him break out in hives. But it felt so good to see somebody besides Papa. Papa, whose eyes had deep circles underneath them, like he had the flu. Because of me. All because of me.

"How are we going to do this project, Ty?" Casey asked. "I brought a tree guide along. You want to start at the beginning?"

"You don't need a book with me around," I bragged. "I know every tree in our woods by name."

"What? Michael the maple? Sam the sycamore? Here's Polly the pine tree. How are your needles today?"

I scowled at him. "Okay, so I was showing off. But just a little. Let's go into the woods and find all the trees we can."

We set off across the backyard toward the woods. A morning chill still hung in the air, but the day would heat up soon. The shade in the woods would feel good.

"Tyler, you sure we'll get all twenty trees? That Ms. Custer doesn't believe in starting off the year slow, does she?" He reached up to pull a leaf off a sugar maple. "Where do we get the bark? I heard it hurts the tree if you cut off the bark."

I reached for a low branch and pulled myself up. "If I find a dead limb, I'll rip bark off that," I said. "You want to try the same thing with that pin oak over there?"

"This one? Sure, I'll try it."

I watched Casey scramble up that oak tree like a frisky squirrel.

I stuck maple leaves and bark in my bag and slid down to the ground. A sumac grew nearby, and I didn't mind cutting a hunk of live bark off that tree. Sumacs are junk trees, springing up wherever there's open space. Papa always hacks them down to give the good trees room.

"Hey, this is a birch, right, Ty? This loose bark is easy to collect."

"So is sycamore," I told him. "Bark falls off as the tree grows. We're doing great."

And we were—for the science project. I wasn't sure about anything else. I wiped sweat off my forehead and wished for just a moment that I could wipe away everything Papa had told me the night before.

I moved to a blue spruce, twisted off a small bunch of needles, and searched the ground for loose bark and a cone or two.

"Hey, great. You got a pine!" Casey shouted. "We'll be done before you know it."

"Spruce," I corrected. "There's a stand of pines ahead, and cedar trees near the house."

"Sorry, tree wizard," he said. "I'm just a dumb kid who thinks trees are for climbing."

"Come on, Casey, you're writing up our report. I'm in charge of the trees. We agreed already."

"Yeah. I know. You're the tree wizard. Add my amazing hand with Magic Markers, and those other kids don't have a chance. You think she'll give extra credit if we get more than twenty trees?"

"Worth a try," I said. "We can make a poster. The evergreens. Needles and cones. And bark."

"Rarrf, rarrf, rarrf!"

"Casey, what are you doing?"

"You said *bark*. I was barking."

I rolled my eyes. "I was talking about a poster, Case. With bark. Tree bark," I added fast, so he wouldn't start up again like a hound dog in pain.

He stuck out his tongue and panted, just to let me know he'd rarrf again if I gave him an excuse. Then he returned to human speech. "Okay. We'll make a poster. I'm making a poster for my family tree, too. Old Ms. Custer has trees on the brain. How's yours coming? Your family tree?"

"Watch out! That's poison ivy you're reaching for, Casey," I snapped. "Don't you know anything?"

His hand flew back from the glossy green leaves like it had wings. "Geez, Ty. What bee stung your butt?"

Casey's bottom lip stuck out. I had to apologize. It wasn't his fault he didn't know his way around the woods. Even more, it wasn't his fault that he'd accidentally stepped into the tangle of my worries.

"Sorry, Case," I said.

My face must have shown something. Casey got nice, real fast.

"Hey, Ty. She's a mean teacher. She gave us a truckload of work, and it's just the first week of school. I got a headache from all the long division." He punched my shoulder. "I'll help design your family tree. I have fifty good ideas, and I can use only one myself."

My eyes filled up, and I turned away. I wasn't quick enough. Casey pulled on my arm.

"Hey, what is it? Don't let her get to you, Tyler. You're good in school. You're twice as good as me in math. You'll do okay on these tree things."

I shook my head. It was no use. Water flooded my eyes faster than I could blink it away. "I can't do it, Casey. I don't have a family tree. After what Papa told me last night, I don't even have a family."

"Hey," he said again. "What do you mean, no family?"

Casey's brown eyes had a soft look in them, like he was talking to a hurt puppy. I guess he was. Papa wasn't the only one who'd lost sleep.

"It's like this," I said. "I don't have a family, I can't make a family tree, and I'm going to flunk sixth grade. I'm not even the person I thought I was yesterday. Everything's upside down."

"So tell Ms. Custer," he said, his voice soft and easy.

"I can't," I wailed. "I can't explain anything to her."

Casey reached into his backpack for two juice cans. He passed me one. "What's going on?"

My breath caught then, like it does when you've been crying for a long time or when you're scared. The things Papa had told me were chewing me up inside. I had to talk it out.

"Can you keep a secret?" I demanded.

He nodded.

"Promise?"

"You know me, Tyler. I don't spill private stuff."

I took a deep breath to clear the wobblies out of my voice. "Casey," I began, "what do you know about the Amish?"

Chapter 6

As I told Casey he didn't say much except the occasional "wow" or "no way." I told everything at least twice.

We got back to the house in time for lunch. Papa had set out the last of the cold ham, and we built big sandwiches. I was hungrier than I'd thought—either that or I ate fast because I had nothing to say.

After we finished the food, we got out our leaves and bark and sorted them into piles. I folded each tree's stuff into a piece of newspaper and wrote the name on the outside. Casey would take the packets home and put each tree on its own page. We'd found a big hunk of birch bark to

41

use for the cover, so when he finished all the fancy printing, I'd sew it into a book. Then he'd make the evergreen poster and we'd get an A-plus for sure.

I helped him load the tree stuff into his backpack. "Call if you need anything," I said. "If a leaf gets torn or we forgot some bark."

"I will." He swung his leg over the bike. "And Tyler, that other tree thing. The family one. I thought about it all through lunch."

"Yeah?" I held my breath, waiting. What did he think about me, now that he knew who I really was?

"You've got two choices with old Ms. Custer. Tell her the whole story like you told me, or make it all up. Either way, I'll help."

"You mean lie?" Sure, I'd planned to lie, but somehow it sounded worse when Casey said it out loud. It made me feel like a criminal.

He shrugged. "Doesn't matter to me, Tyler. Where your family came from, that's your business. But some people might not see it that way."

When he said "some people," I thought of Sissy Norman's face with an ugly grin plastered across the mouth.

I shook my head. It was too much to think about. I raised my hand to wave to Casey.

"Do a good job with our tree stuff," I called to him. "Be careful."

"Leaf it to me," he called back. Then he laughed and barked some more, yowling all the way down the driveway.

Papa came into the kitchen late in the afternoon, smelling of fresh sawdust. "You had a good time in the woods this morning, *ja?*"

"Yes, Papa. We collected stuff for school."

"*Ja.* School." He took my chin in his hand and tipped my face up so he could look right into my eyes. "This other schoolwork takes your sleep, daughter?"

He asked it like a question, so I nodded. I might have to lie to Ms. Custer but not to Papa. Never to Papa.

"*Ja.* I was awake in the night, too. I did some big thinking."

I smiled.

"I carried a trunk today, Tyler. While you and your friend hunted for trees, I went to the attic and brought down some things for you. You're old enough now."

I knew what he was talking about, even without his telling me.

"Your mama's things," he said. "I packed them up for you a long time ago. Books and quilts and music."

Books and quilts, that made sense. But music? "What music?"

"You remember the tape machine?" A small smile twitched at the corners of his mouth.

I grinned back. "How could I forget?"

For a moment, all thoughts of Mama and the Amish and family trees flew from my head, and I was back in kindergarten again with the flower teacher. Once she had made it clear she wasn't in line to be my next mama, Ms. Holden took a special interest in me. She'd told Papa I needed to work on my English, and she lent me books and tapes with stories to listen to. She suggested that I watch television, but Papa said no, that was too modern. *Modern nonsense* were the exact words he'd used, I think.

"I agree with you about television," the teacher had said. "But surely she can hear stories on tape. You have a tape player?"

"*Ja.* We got a tape machine."

That had brought me out of my chair. I never knew we had a tape player. But sure enough, once we got home, Papa disappeared for a while and returned with a tape recorder for me to use.

I'd pestered him, but he never told me where he got that machine. I'd never guessed it came from Mama.

"Will you mind if I listen to her music?" I asked now.

"You can listen, Tyler. But don't play it too loud. I'm not sure I can listen to her songs, even now."

I threw my arms around him then, to thank him for this gift and also to soften the hurt in his eyes. "Might be fun to listen to a song, Papa. Might bring back the good times."

He shrugged and tried a smile. "Could be," he said. "Give me a little more time, *liebchen*."

Chapter 7

The trunk sat in my room under the window like it belonged there. Like it filled up a space that had been empty for a long time. I ran my fingers over the curved wooden top and felt the cool iron bands that held it together.

I took a deep breath. Most of my life I'd wished for a mother. I needed to do this right. To be careful and not hurry.

I opened the hasp and lifted the lid. Beautiful colors swam in front of my eyes. I blinked a few times, and the colors arranged themselves into the pieces of a quilt. Red flowers, green leaves. I lifted the quilt with both hands and unfolded it on my bed. It fit just right.

Had she made it herself? I stared at the quilt

again, examining the bold pattern and the tiny stitches. Then in one corner I saw initials. *BJK.* Someone else had made this quilt. Mama had loved it, so she'd bought it. Maybe she'd even bought it for me. For the new baby she was expecting.

I went back to the trunk and picked up a shoebox. When I lifted the lid, I saw a row of tape cases. Mama's music. Beatles tapes, and Rolling Stones. Oldies for me, but music from her time. Music she'd liked. Imagine. Now I could play Beatles songs. All of them, from the looks of the shoebox.

Another shoebox held more tapes. Classical. Mozart and Beethoven, Brahms and Chopin. I pulled some tapes out. She'd liked piano music and string quartets. I bet I'd like them, too.

At the bottom of the trunk I found books. I was used to finding Mama's books. Downstairs in the living room, we had shelves filled with books. Novels and biographies and histories. Her name, Sarah Tyler, was written on the first page of nearly every one. But these books were different. They were still wearing their dust jackets, and they looked new.

My fingers shook as I lifted out the first book. Sure enough, one of *her* books. One she'd written herself. *A Simple Story: Everyday Life Among the Shakers of New York.* I found three copies of the Shaker book. All brand-new. And underneath were her other books, too.

I forced my hands to be careful as I lifted out the books. Later I'd read each one and try to imagine my mother sitting down at her typewriter to write. But at that moment there was one book I wanted, *needed* to find.

Yes. Here. Four copies. *A Plain Wedding: The Courtship and Marriage of an Amish Woman.*

I opened the book to the first page and read the dedication. *To Dorcas Stoudt and her family, who have taught me much about loving. S.T.*

Dorcas Stoudt. Papa's sister. I held Papa's family in my hands. Papa's family in Mama's words.

I took a deep breath and turned the page.

Love sits gently on the shoulders of Dorcas Stoudt. It deepens the brown of her eyes. It plants a shy smile on her lips. It brushes her cheek with warm color.

Dorcas Stoudt is a plain woman, a member of an Amish community near Lancaster, Pennsylvania. But no woman in love is ever plain. Dorcas has just become engaged to her childhood sweetheart, and joy shines in her face. . . .

I touched my fingers to the words on the page. Mama.

Mama was telling me about my aunt Dorcas in the years before I was born. Later I'd go back. I'd read the book over and over and write down all the names I found. I'd grow myself a family tree from the names in this book.

Mama's words filled my head Saturday afternoon and all day Sunday as well. The story was Papa's. His sister Dorcas. His father, Titus, his mother, Rachel. And the history of the Amish people in America, how they'd been persecuted for their religious beliefs and come to America to escape. Papa's history. Papa's people.

But the words were Mama's. And through the words I learned how thoughtful Mama was. How she had understood people who seemed different. How she had treated their lives and their traditions with honor and respect. I wished then, for about the millionth time, that she were still around to teach me those things and everything else she knew.

Chapter 8

Sissy Norman caught me by surprise when I walked into school on Monday morning. She had one of those cardboard mailing tubes in her hand, and she was making a big deal of opening the end as I dropped my book bag on my desk, right behind her.

"Turns out I'm French," she said with a toss of her head. She'd arranged her dark hair in a perfect French braid, probably in honor of her family's history. "See? A fleur-de-lis border." She pointed to the edge of her chart.

I peeked over at the paper. Big mistake. Double mistake, really. First my stomach flipped over, once I realized that Sissy and probably the rest of the kids had their family trees ready to hand in, and I didn't even have the paper anymore. I'd wadded up the two halves after Papa tore the paper up. I'd hidden the pieces deep in the trash can.

The second bad thing was Sissy. She caught me looking. "I'm French," she repeated. "And my family came to America a long, long time ago. What about you, Tyler? Where are your ancestors from?"

I had part of an answer now, thanks to Mama's book. But before I could open my mouth, Casey Powell rushed over.

"You're French?" he demanded. "Ooh-la-la. Speak to me, *mademoiselle*!" He shook his hips, and I was afraid he might dance the cancan right between the desks.

"I *am* French," Sissy shot back. "My last name is just like in Normandy. And my real first name is Cecile."

"You're about as French as a french fry," he said. "And I bet your last name comes from Norman's Used Cars, over in Smithville."

"Who asked you, Casey Powell?" Sissy's eyes looked ready to shoot lightning.

"Ladies. Gentlemen. Might I have an explanation, please?"

Ms. Custer's voice cut through the argument like one of Papa's sharp saws through pine. I swallowed hard. Even though I wasn't actually fighting, I was part of it. Casey had gone after Sissy because he knew I was touchy about my family tree. I edged closer to his desk.

"Casey says I'm not French and I am," Sissy complained.

The teacher nodded. "Casey, what do you have to say for yourself?"

"Um," he mumbled. "Not much, ma'am."

That was Casey. He never tattled.

"Sissy was—" I began.

"I am too French," Sissy interrupted. She turned on Casey and me. "My family goes back years and years." Her cheeks reddened, and she was close to tears.

"Casey," Ms. Custer said. "Why were you and Sissy arguing?"

Casey's face turned bright red, too. "I don't know. It's weird. Maybe a long time ago some guy in her family did come from France. But that doesn't make her French. She's American, just like me. The way she was talking, you'd think she was related to one of those rich old kings or queens."

"You can't prove I'm not," Sissy snapped.

Ms. Custer looked from Casey to Sissy and back again. "This is excellent," she said, smiling. "We're going to have a wonderful year together."

I grabbed hold of my desk to keep from falling over. Kids had warned us that Ms. Custer was mean and strict, but nobody'd ever said she was crazy. I stared right at her face. What was going on?

Scott, the kid next to me, made a mark on the back cover of a notebook. Since the second day of school he'd been keeping track of how many times our teacher said *excellent*. He'd filled one whole row and started the second.

"You two got right to the heart of things," Ms. Custer went on. "Being an American is all about being different. Different histories, different roots, different families. And yes, different opinions. Arguing about things. You've brought those differences out in the open about a week sooner than any other class I've ever taught. Congratulations." She stopped talking and shook both Sissy's and Casey's hands. Both kids gave her back fish-eye stares and waited.

She leaned back against a nearby desk and spoke again. The rest of the class gathered around to watch like it was a fight on the playground.

"Casey, you raise an issue we'll discuss again and again. By the end of the year, you will know a great deal about the other continents on our earth. You will have a better understanding of your own country as well. Sissy, you have your family tree in front of you. Help us get started. Tell us more about your French ancestors."

Sissy beamed Casey and me an I-told-you-so look. She pointed to her chart. "My ancestors came here in the seventeen hundreds," she said. "French Huguenots. That's a kind of Protestant. France was a Catholic country. They gave the Huguenots a hard time. Even killed them. So my ancestors escaped to America."

I couldn't believe what I was hearing. Sissy's ancestors and mine had done the same thing! It was all there in Mama's book. I snapped my lips shut before I blurted that out, though. No way could I tell about being Amish.

Ms. Custer strode to the front of the room and wrote in large letters on the blackboard *To escape religious persecution*. "Has anyone else discovered an ancestor who came to America to worship in freedom?"

I chewed my bottom lip.

"My grandparents," said a voice from the back of the room. Everybody turned to look. Michael Cohen.

"They came from Germany. Because of Hitler. He was wiping out the Jews and everybody else who didn't agree with him. So it was religion, but it was other stuff, too. Politics."

"Political oppression," Ms. Custer said, nodding. She wrote that on the board under *religious persecution*. "Anyone else have a family member who came to America to escape political oppression?"

A hand went up on the side of the room by the windows. Mimi Deng. "I was born here, but my family came from South Vietnam," she said in a soft voice. "During and after the war many people were killed. We were lucky. My family escaped."

I stared at her. I knew Mimi Deng. I'd even known that her family was Vietnamese. Just like I'd known about Michael Cohen being Jewish. But I hadn't known they had stories to tell, about parents and grandparents escaping from another country.

I looked around the room, wondering what other stories I would hear. Most everybody looked like ordinary Americans, even me. But looks weren't everything—people and families had secrets.

I did. I sure didn't feel ordinary. I was the only kid in the class who didn't have a TV or a radio at home. The only one who still got homegrown haircuts and mostly homegrown food. My eyes

55

took in Mimi's face and hairstyle and pretty clothes. I was probably the only girl there who'd never owned a fancy dress or hair ribbons or—

"Yes indeed." Ms. Custer's voice interrupted my wondering. "An excellent beginning," she said.

Scott scratched another mark on his notebook.

"As the weeks go on, we'll discover other reasons for coming to this country. Meanwhile, I'd like someone to prepare a chart for the class. Country of origin, reason for leaving, time of leaving, and so on. Sissy, perhaps you'll volunteer. You've done a lovely job with your family tree."

"Sure. I guess so."

"And Casey?" the teacher asked. "Want to give Sissy a hand?"

I knew what Ms. Custer was up to. She wanted to get Sissy and Casey to stop fighting by making them work together on a project. Teachers always pulled that.

Casey nodded to Ms. Custer. Then he turned and shot me a ferocious scowl. He knew what Ms. Custer wanted, too.

I felt bad. I'd gotten him into this. I couldn't leave him there alone. I stuck my hand up and said, "I'll help, too, Ms. Custer."

"Excellent. Thank you, Tyler."

Scott added another mark to his *excellent* chart and grinned.

I didn't feel like grinning, though. And I didn't think the day was going to be excellent for anybody but Ms. Custer. I'd just stuck myself with Sissy Norman. That could wreck a month.

Then the day got a lot worse. "Pass in your family trees, please," Ms. Custer said. "And find page fifteen in your math books."

Casey groaned out loud at the word *math*.

I turned around to collect the papers from the kid behind me. I rattled the pages to make it sound like I had something to pass in. I might have fooled Sissy, who swung herself around to grab the bunch of papers. But it was Ms. Custer, not Sissy, I had to worry about.

The kid hadn't been born yet who could fool Ms. Custer.

Chapter 9

"**A** re you adopted, Tyler?"

The teacher's words froze my tongue into a solid block of ice. She'd made me come in after lunch to discuss something. The *something* was my family tree. The one I hadn't passed in.

"Are you adopted, dear?" She patted my hand as she asked her question again.

I shook my head. "No, ma'am. My father is my real father, and my mother . . . she died when I was born."

"I start each year with the family tree unit," she explained. "I try to find out before school starts if any of my students are adopted. Teacher grapevine, you know. If a student is adopted, I discuss the project with her in advance so she can decide how she wishes to proceed. Saves embarrassment. Since you didn't hand in a family tree, I wondered if perhaps I had slipped up. . . ."

Her words drifted off, and it was my turn to talk next. I wanted to lie, but something in Ms. Custer's face stopped me.

"I didn't hand in a family tree," I began. "Until this weekend I didn't know much about my family. Papa never talks about it. He just says our family is long gone. It makes him upset. So I don't ask anymore. When I told him about the family tree last Friday, he ripped up the paper."

"Oh dear," Ms. Custer said.

"It's okay. All the stuff I wrote down on that sheet was wrong. Papa isn't German and Mama wasn't English."

I rushed in then with the rest of the story. I even told her the Amish part. I didn't want Papa to look bad for ripping up the chart. I couldn't blame him, not after hearing how his family had cut him off. I hoped Ms. Custer would understand.

She did.

"We'll work out another assignment for you, Tyler," she suggested. "There's always a country or a region with no one to represent it. You can take over that area."

I thought about it for a minute. I could become

an expert on Australia. Nobody in our whole town came from Australia. But it didn't feel right.

"I'd like to do my own tree, if I can. I found out neat stuff about Papa's family from my mother's book. It's fifteen years old, but I can figure out most of my relatives. I just need more time."

"Time's not a problem. I suppose your mother's family is much less of a mystery, thank goodness."

I chewed on my lip. "Actually, I don't even know their names," I said. "Papa and I have lived by ourselves. Do I need both sides of the family to pass?"

There. It was out. The big question. Would I make it through the sixth grade or would I flunk?

Ms. Custer patted my hand like I was a little kid. "You do the best you can, Tyler. Do the best you can, and you'll be fine. Get your father's family down on paper and then come talk to me again. We'll see what we can do about those *English* ancestors of yours."

You do the best you can, Tyler. Do the best you can, and you'll be fine. . . .

Those dumb words stuck with me all day, like a tune you can't get out of your head. Part of me wished Ms. Custer had been mean and nasty, like she was supposed to be. Then I could have scribbled off any old family tree and made up for my bad grade on the next project. But since she'd been nice, I didn't want to let her down. I had to do my very best.

I started first thing when I got home from school. Papa was still in his shop, so I had the dining room table all to myself. No point working on something hurtful with Papa around. If I hurried, he wouldn't even have to look at it.

I went through Mama's book again, this time looking for names and ages. Not an easy job. Papa had ten brothers and sisters. Ten! I figured them all out. Using Papa's birthday, then subtracting or adding, I got the birth years. I wrote down the names of his parents and grandparents. Mama's book only went back that far, but it was a start.

As I leafed through, I found the place where Mama first talked about Papa in her book. Maybe Papa didn't know, but I could tell that they'd fall in love.

. . . The oldest brother, Reuben, is like oldest brothers everywhere. He's smart, works hard, and tries to advise the rest of the family about how to behave. The second brother, Jakob, is a sweet man. He speaks in a gentle voice, and when Reu-

ben teases Dorcas or his other sisters too long, Jakob runs interference.

One evening at supper, Reuben brought up locking the windows and doors. "Seems we've had a young man in the house," he said. "It's too late to keep Dorcas at home. That Timothy Miller has stolen her heart. But it's not too late to lock out other young men who might come to call."

[Note: For some Amish, courting is a secret ritual. The young man has to sneak into the girl's home after everyone else is asleep to woo her. If Reuben installed locks, his younger sisters would find their suitors locked out.]

"Reuben, you can't," Lisbet protested. "I'm only one year younger than Dorcas. And Ruth and Leah are right behind me."

"Ach. Babies, all of you. Ja, I think we need some nice strong iron locks. Two, three years at least."

The sisters discussed it with Reuben, in a good-natured way at first. But he kept teasing, and Lisbet's cheeks began to redden.

Then Jakob spoke up, smiling at his sister. "Ach, Lisbet. Don't listen to this old rooster. You know Reuben as well as I do, and I ask you, will our brother really want to spend good money for *locks when he doesn't have to? Count up all the windows and doors!"*

Laughter bubbled around the table then. The sisters smiled, and even Reuben wore a grin as if to say, I was joking all along. . . .

I could almost see myself sitting at the table with those sisters . . . no, those aunts. I ran my fingers across the page, touching the words. Mama's words, smooth as any board Papa ever sanded. Was this as close as I'd ever get to having a family?

I must have sat there for a long time, because the next thing I knew, the back door creaked. Papa. Papa was coming in for supper.

Papa was coming in for supper, and I hadn't even started to cook. I reached for my papers and notes. If I could gather them up and hide Mama's book . . .

"*Ach,* Tyler. Working so hard for your new teacher. You're a good girl."

"I forgot to start supper," I mumbled. If he'd only go upstairs to wash, I could put everything inside a notebook.

But he stopped next to the table and picked up a sheet of paper. "You're building your tree, aren't you, Tyler?"

"Yes, Papa." I looked down at my hands.

"There's a mistake here, daughter. Dorcas was born in 1955. You put down 1956. Where did you get these numbers?"

My fingers curled into fists. "Sorry, Papa. I didn't want to bother you. I . . . I just took your birthday and figured out your brothers and sisters. I can't do that for my gra— for your parents. But I'll do the best I can."

"I'll help," he said, messing my hair with his big hand. "If the window is open an inch or a foot, cold air still blows in. *Ja,* I'll help."

Chapter 10

"You said you didn't start supper yet, *liebchen?*"

"No, Papa. I'm sorry. I . . . I forgot."

"There's plenty of daylight left; let's catch us a supper. You put the books away, I dig some worms. *Ja?*"

We walked to the lake, scuffing through old leaves. Papa carried a can of worms and an empty pail for the fish. I swung two poles on my shoulder.

Papa picked out a spot on our favorite flat rock, and we sat down and got to work. We didn't talk much when we went fishing. It scared the fish. Besides, we'd fished together forever, so I knew what to do. Bait the hook, drop it lightly into the water. Wait. And watch.

The rock felt warm from the sun, and below, the water caught the sun's light like diamonds. I watched my line and Papa's, glad we didn't have to talk for a while.

Something moved. The sunlight flickered on a shape below the water. Dinner, if we were lucky.

Papa caught the first perch. I caught two more. He cleaned them right there and tossed the insides to an old crow that guarded our rock from a nearby tree. The crow went to work, like those fish guts were a feast.

Papa washed off his hands and his knife in the lake. He rinsed the pail and tossed in the cleaned fish.

Across the water, I heard the low call of a mourning dove. I scanned the trees, looking for her.

"*Ja*. I see her," Papa said. He pointed off to the right. "High up in that wild cherry tree. See, Tyler?"

I looked and listened. When she called again, I saw her. She must have seen me, too, because she scolded and flew away.

"See that bird's tail?" Papa said. He took a wet

finger and drew the shape on our rock. "It's how I make my corners fit. A dove's tail. On a drawer. Or the edge of a shelf. Dove's-tail joint, it's called."

I looked at the shapes on the rock. I remembered those shapes from his workshop. Remembered watching Papa carve out the tails of the doves.

"Makes a nice tight fit, Tyler. You carve it right, you don't even need glue. The wood holds together real good. I use glue, though. To be safe. Don't want my furniture to fall apart, no matter what."

The dove called again, and I watched her fly across the sky. I especially watched her tail, wondering who had ever thought up the idea of using a dove's-tail shape to make pieces of wood fit together.

"Too bad," Papa said. His voice got soft and quiet. "Too bad our family isn't made like that dove's-tail joint. Made so it fits together nice and tight. Our family fell apart like a cheap chair. Not enough glue in this world to make the Stoudts all stick together again."

"Oh, Papa. I'm sorry. You don't have to remember this. It's too hard."

"Hard. Living it was hard. *Ja*. Remembering is

not so bad." He stood and gathered up the fish pail and the bait can. I grabbed the poles and followed him on the path toward home.

"I'll cook the fish, Papa. Nice and crispy and brown." Anything to change the subject. "And tomatoes, and beans."

"*Ja,* Tyler. You cook the fish. Then, after supper, we sit down and fill up your family tree. I want you to do good work in school. You got that strict teacher, you can't skip things."

Ms. Custer. She was strict, all right. She'd made me start this family tree project and get Papa all upset. But if I was honest, I had to admit something. Ms. Custer wasn't the only one getting Papa upset. I shared the blame. Ms. Custer had offered me a way out, and I hadn't taken it. So whatever happened next was partly my fault.

We did the dishes together. I washed, Papa dried. Afterward we sat at the kitchen table. Name by name, date by date, Papa gave me my family tree.

The beginning was the hardest. His voice cracked when he told me the names of his brothers and sisters, his parents. It made my heart sore to hear him pronounce *Dorcas, Levi, Reuben*, and the rest in a heavy accent. By the time we got to his aunts and uncles and grandparents, I was sure the worst was over. He even smiled when he told me how his two grandmothers, Ruth Stoudt and Hannah Yoder, both had wanted to be the best pie bakers in Lancaster County.

"*Ja,* I got lots of pies to taste," he chuckled. "I made sure to take a long time to decide which was best. Two, three pieces sometimes to decide."

When we'd gone back as far as he could remember, he took my hand and squeezed it. "You got a family now, Tyler. At least in writing you got a family."

I smiled at him and wriggled the fingers of my right hand to ease the stiffness. Amish families had lots of kids, so my family tree had a million branches. I liked knowing that somewhere there were lots of Stoudts, even if I didn't know them personally. And with all those names, Ms. Custer would pass me for sure.

"Thanks, Papa. I know it was hard. . . ."

"*Ja,* hard. But it is good to know where you come from, yes, Tyler?"

"Yes, Papa." And because he said that, because it did feel good to know, I plunged on. "But I don't know anything about the Tylers. What do you know about them? Is Mama's family dead?"

"I used to wish they were," he said. "Those Tylers! Bad, bad people. I shunned them!"

"What?" I said. I looked into his eyes and saw anger, dark and cold.

"They did not want me as husband for their daughter, their only child. The father called names at me. Acted like he was king and I was his servant."

I was afraid to ask what names. It was too horrible. I didn't really want to know.

Papa went on, "When I marry your mother, we go to their house. We argue. Your mother and I leave quick. Soon we come here to live. We put many miles between us and those Tylers."

"Did Mama ever see her parents after that? Did she stay mad?"

"Your mama, she wrote letters to her mama. Called on the telephone. She made some visits when the father was not at home. I never went. I only saw those Tylers two times. Two bad times." He shook his head, as if it hurt just thinking about Mama's parents. "The second time was the funeral," he whispered. "They came here when your mother died." Papa's eyes glistened, but he wasn't angry now, only sad.

But me, I was angry enough for both of us.

"They came here and saw us when Mama died and that's it? Okay, I understand. They were mad at you. But what did I ever do? Why were they mad at me?"

"Mad? At you, Tyler? Nobody got mad at you. You were just a baby."

"But they never came back. They're my grandparents, and they never even sent me a card or a letter. They acted like I died with Mama."

"*Ja*. That is how they act." Papa looked away from me. He turned so his face was sideways, and I could see a frown, a frown and something more.

"That is how they act, *liebchen,* because that is what they think. Your mama, she died a long time before you were due. So I let them think you died too. I never told them you were born."

"Papa!"

The word roared from my throat so loud and so hard it hurt.

"Papa! How could you?"

"For you, *liebchen*. For you. And . . . and yes. For me. I was afraid they would take you from me so I hid the truth. You were very small. And the hospital for tiny babies. It was far away from here. Cleveland. Too far for them to find out about. So I took the easy road. I let them think you died with your mother. I hope you can forgive me." Papa still wouldn't look me in the eye but I understood what I'd seen in his face. He was ashamed.

And he deserved to be!

I didn't trust myself to say a single word. I shoved back my chair and raced upstairs. I banged my bedroom door so hard a book fell from the shelf. I threw myself onto the bed and pounded my pillow as tears came, hot, scalding tears.

But the tears were nothing compared to my temper. I boiled and raged and fumed.

I'd never forgive Papa for this. *Never.*

Chapter 11

"I figured it all out," Sissy announced the next morning when I arrived at school. "You're in charge of the maps, Tyler." She plunked a thick book and a box of paper on my desk.

"What?"

"The maps. I brought tracing paper and an atlas. You get to draw the maps."

"Which maps, Sissy?"

"The ones we're going to put the stickers on, of course. I'm doing the stickers."

"The stickers?"

I probably sounded like a parrot, repeating every word Sissy said. But I had no idea what she was talking about.

"Look, Tyler. You make maps of each country. I

make stickers for every kid in the class. We put the sticker on the right map and *zap,* our project is done. Simple."

"Gotta be simple if you thought it up, Sissy." Casey came up behind us. He stared at the stuff she'd brought. "What's my part?"

"And how come I have to make all the maps?" I demanded. "There are hundreds of countries in the world!" I could hear my voice get loud, but it felt good to holler at somebody.

"Look. This is all planned. You're trying to wreck it," Sissy snapped.

Casey shook his head. "Come off it, French Fry. What did you do besides raid your mom's desk for stickers and tracing paper? We're working on this together. That means we all decide stuff. Together."

She stuck her nose in the air and marched off to the pencil sharpener.

I sighed. This was all my fault.

"So what are we going to do?" I asked Casey. "Her idea isn't so bad."

"We'll use parts of her idea. The stickers sound good."

Sissy came back scowling. "*If* I let you use my stickers."

Ms. Custer called for order then, and we stood

up to say the Pledge of Allegiance: . . . *one nation, under God, indivisible, with liberty and justice for all.*

I was so mixed up, the familiar words comforted me. I paid extra attention that morning, and as I listened I realized something. I didn't understand much about my country, and I wanted to. I wanted to figure out how a bunch of people from lots of different places came to a new land and managed to live together without too much fighting.

Papa had sure fought with those Tylers. Casey and I and Sissy Norman lived only a few miles apart, and we fussed like chickens.

I stared at her. From looking at the back of her French-braided head and her stiff shoulders, I could tell Sissy was crabby. Crabbier than a wet cat.

By afternoon, Sissy and I had both cooled off. Ms. Custer gave us time to work on the project when we finished our vocabulary sheets.

"I like your idea about the stickers and the maps," I began, trying to keep her good mood from flying out the window. "But I'm not the world's best artist. We need a copying machine. I'll ask Ms. Custer."

"I guess so," Sissy agreed.

"I like your idea, too," Casey chimed in.

I shot him a grin. He was doing better.

"But there's more neat stuff we can do," he said. "How many kids' families came to America to get away from something bad, like religious or political persecution? My family came here for land. They were farmers, and the land in Ireland all belonged to the big shots. Also there was a potato famine, so they were hungry."

"I don't think we can put all that on a map," Sissy said. She frowned. "There won't be room."

"How about a chart, like Ms. Custer said?" Casey suggested. "Your maps show where people came from, and I make a chart about why and when."

"Might work," Sissy agreed slowly. "We'll need at least two answers for each kid. One for the mother's side and one for the father's. That means extra stickers and big charts."

"No problem," Casey said. "The bigger the better." He grinned. He'd had this stuff in mind all along and was pleased with himself.

I looked out the window and scowled. Nice for Casey. He'd dreamed up good ideas and figured out how to convince Sissy. But her words reminded me of my own chart—the family tree

Papa had helped me work on the night before, after we came in from the lake.

Except for the last fifteen years, I now had all the dates and names to complete the Stoudt family tree. Papa had said, *Your tree is your ancestors. Your roots. The past doesn't change. So who needs all those new cousins?*

I pushed away the memory. My eyes fogged, and I blinked hard. I wouldn't cry in school. I couldn't! And besides, what was there to cry about? A bunch of people I'd never met? Cousins who wore old-fashioned bonnets and long dresses? Or had my eyes filled up because of the sad way Papa had sounded when he said all those names? Reuben and Joseph, Leah and Ruth. The baby, Levi.

I watched a pair of swallows swoop and dart across the sky outside the window, and I took a deep breath. To be truthful, I could have cried about all those things. But the big thing, the hardest of all, was the other side of the tree. One whole branch I knew nothing about.

The Tylers.

Worse, they knew nothing about me.

Chapter 12

I slipped the Stoudt family tree onto Ms. Custer's desk that afternoon, on my way out to the bus. I found it the next morning inside my desk with a note attached.

Good work so far, Tyler. See me during recess after lunch. Ms. Custer.

I still couldn't think of a way to snoop about Mama's family. I sure wouldn't ask Papa again. I'd barely spoken to him for two nights. Every time I remembered what he'd told me, I got the shivers.

Somehow I shoved the worries aside long enough to get through morning classes. Our first reading book was *The Witch of Blackbird Pond*. It wasn't too hard to guess why. Ms. Custer wanted us to figure out what it felt like to be hassled for being different.

The story scared me. What if kids found out Papa was Amish, not just German? People might get nasty. All the more reason to keep my mouth shut.

I wished things were different. Wished Papa hadn't lied. Wished I were a regular girl, like Sissy Norman, who always knew what to wear and how to please the teachers. Wished Mama had lived to teach me those things.

I didn't talk much during lunch. I let my mind wander while Casey complained about having to check and recheck all the multiplication and long division by hand.

"It's bad enough she makes us do all those problems, but then we have to undo them. Pages and pages. Hasn't she ever heard of calculators?"

"Uh-huh," I agreed. Somehow Casey's complaining was a comfort to me. It was a regular part of knowing Casey. No surprises. Nothing scary. I was glad to let his voice rattle on. Then two other voices started from the table behind me, and I couldn't help but hear what they said.

"I have cousins in California," Mimi Deng said. "It costs a lot of money for airplane tickets, so we can't go visit except once a year. Then it's like a party. I have sixteen cousins and lots of aunts and uncles. You should see all the food. . . ."

"I know what you mean," Jasmine Williams said. "For us it's like that every summer. We go to North Carolina and we eat for two weeks straight. It's the Williams family reunion. They've been doing it since long before I was born. All I had to do for my family tree was get out the old pictures and start writing. Mom has these scrapbooks. She even sent copies of the tree I made to all her sisters and brothers."

"Great idea," Mimi said. "I could send mine to my cousins for presents."

I felt a lump grow in my throat. All this talk about family reunions and cousins . . . It would be a present to me if I had a picture or even the name of just one cousin.

I balled up my lunch bag and headed for the trash cans. "See you after recess," I told Casey. "I have to go talk to Ms. Custer."

"Maybe you can talk her out of giving us math homework," he suggested. "Give my poor old brain a night off."

"Right," I said. But I could understand what he meant. My head was tired, too, but not from math problems.

80

"You worked quickly, Tyler. Your chart is nearly complete, and you have a very large family."

The room was empty except for my teacher and me. Everyone else was outside playing. Ms. Custer borrowed Casey's chair and pulled it over to my desk. She examined my family tree.

"I don't have any information about changes in my father's family since he left Pennsylvania," I said. "I don't know about cousins or new aunts and uncles by marriage."

"You have your ancestors, though. That's enough for your father's side."

Enough for her, maybe. But not for me. After all that talk at lunch, I could imagine a whole flock of cousins with Papa's accent—girls in long dresses and boys with bowl haircuts.

"What do you know about your mother's people?"

There. The question I'd worried over all morning. I swallowed hard, trying to forget the fire in Papa's eyes when he'd told me about them.

"Mama was an only child," I began. "She came from Massachusetts. I never met her parents. I don't know them at all."

"Do you want to talk about this, Tyler? If it's

private, I won't intrude. You needn't finish this part of your tree for me, you know . . . what you've done so far is plenty."

I studied my teacher's face, trying to decide. I saw flecks of warm gold in her brown eyes; close up, the lines in her face looked more like smile lines than frown ones.

"I better talk to somebody," I said at last. "I don't understand."

I told her what I knew. What Papa had told me in those few harsh sentences. I told her how, when Papa and Mama had gotten married, the Amish weren't the only ones who didn't like it. How Mama's family got mad. They hadn't liked Papa at all.

"Did your mother keep up with her parents after that?" Ms. Custer asked softly. "Or did they stay apart?"

"Mama wrote to them," I said. "She visited a few times. Papa never did. He was too upset. They . . . they knew I was expected," I said, my voice shaking. This was the hardest part. What Papa had done. "But then the accident happened. A truck hit Mama's car. She died in the ambulance on the way to the hospital."

"But the doctors saved you. You're a sort of miracle, aren't you, Tyler?"

"I guess. Papa always said I was a blessing. God's gift to a man who had lost everything. I guess that's why . . ." My throat closed up, and I couldn't finish the sentence.

Ms. Custer just sat there quietly and waited.

I took a deep breath and pushed the words out of my mouth fast, so I wouldn't cry in front of her. "That's why he didn't tell them about me. Because of Mama's accident. . . . I was born two months early. I wasn't very strong so they took me to a special hospital in Cleveland that treats really tiny babies. So I was far away . . . and hardly anybody knew . . . and Papa could keep me hidden until after the funeral. Papa let the Tylers think I died with Mama. Because . . . because he was afraid. He didn't trust them. He thought they'd take me away from him. So he kept me a secret. He kept me a secret from my own grandparents."

Ms. Custer didn't say anything right away. She just patted my hand and looked out the windows. I tried to catch my breath and stop shaking inside.

When she finally turned to look at me again, she said, "You were a motherless baby. He was an outcast Amish man with no knowledge of American law. . . ." Her voice trailed off, as if she were uncertain.

I thought for a moment. Her words made sense

to me. But there was a nagging thought that took hold of my mind then. It took hold and twirled me around until I felt light and dizzy. But I didn't dare say it out loud.

What about now? I thought. *What if they found out about me now?*

Chapter 13

I don't know what started it, whether it was wanting to do a good job for Ms. Custer or just plain nosiness. But once the idea of finding my grandparents stuck itself in my brain, I couldn't chase it away.

I hurried home that afternoon and said a quick hello to Papa. Then I started a list of everything I knew about the Tyler family. Right off, I took down the atlas and looked up South Egremont, Massachusetts. So far away. I closed the atlas and stared out the window. Shoot. I needed my grandparents' first names or their address.

I knew a place to look. I'd read partway through Mama's book about the Shakers, and I'd figured to read about that Mormon woman next.

But if I wanted clues about my Tyler relatives, those books could wait.

I stashed my schoolbooks in my room and headed down the hall. I opened the door to the attic stairs, stepped inside, and closed the door behind me. I had no reason to feel guilty. Papa had given me some of Mama's stuff. So what if I found more? But somehow I couldn't shake the sneaky feeling.

I told myself I was sneaking to save Papa from being hurt. What a puny excuse. Papa wouldn't like my plans. He'd stop me if he found out.

Up in the attic I pulled on the chain, and light shone down on dust and cobwebs. I saw old things, like my baby cradle and high chair. The wooden trunks where Papa put the winter blankets every summer. I saw lots and lots of boxes, too, some dustier than others. I headed toward the dirtiest of the boxes. Anything that belonged to Mama would have at least eleven years of dust on it.

The box I opened had account books inside and old tax papers. They came from when Papa and Mama had first lived in Ohio. Long before my time. Then I looked to the right. I saw a whole row of boxes pushed back into the eaves all by themselves. In front of those boxes a rectangle of floor shone clean, no dust at all. The clean spot matched the size of the trunk Papa had brought to my room.

I knelt down and reached for the nearest box. I found folders, some of them fat with papers and others nearly empty. I lifted out a handful of folders and opened the first one.

My eyes fogged up, and I swiped at them so no tears would spill out and streak the page.

> *Notes on the Hutterites*
>
> *German-speaking Anabaptists—pacifists, communal living*
>
> *Origins—Moravia, sixteenth century, moved to Russian Ukraine, to western U.S. 1874; also western Canada*
>
> *Communities governed by bishops and preachers*
>
> *All things held in common ownership*
>
> *Family life, simple ways, pacifism valued*

I took a minute to figure out what I was reading: notes for a new book Mama had planned to write. But she hadn't gotten the chance. I touched the words, tracing her letters with my finger. Her handwriting looped and dashed across the page, like she'd been writing in a hurry. My finger felt warm just touching the words.

I tucked the folders under my shirt for safekeeping and reclosed the box. I turned off the light and sneaked back downstairs to my room.

Sprawled on my quilt, I studied the page once more and let out my breath. Suddenly, finding clues about my grandparents didn't matter. Because I had a chance to discover more about Mama.

I wanted to read every word and memorize her ideas. But a little nagging voice inside me said, *Slow down. You may find things you shouldn't read. Things that might upset you.*

I didn't listen to that voice. I couldn't. All my life I'd wanted a mother. If I couldn't have her alive and with me, at least I needed to know what sort of woman she'd been. So I spent the time between school and supper reading. Reading about unusual religions and communal societies. That first afternoon, I read her plans and new ideas.

I didn't finish every folder that day. I read slowly. Every word. Sometimes I read the whole folder twice. And when I finished each folder, I hid it in the trunk under the music tapes and the published books. By suppertime, when I went downstairs to heat up the vegetable soup, I knew something new. Something to be proud of. I, too, was interested in all different sorts of people. I felt curious about how they lived their lives—just like my mother.

I was very much like my mother. I'd only touched the surface of her life so far. I'd read the top layer. But like an archaeologist, I'd dig down to the very bottom of those boxes upstairs. I'd read every word and discover everything I could about the wonderful woman who had been my mother.

Chapter 14

Weird, the way things happen. You can look everywhere for something and not find it. Then the minute you stop looking, the thing finds you.

I had a hard time paying attention to homework with Mama's papers upstairs. But I didn't want to get behind. Ms. Custer had been nice to me so far, and I wanted to keep it that way. So I sat at the table and worked endless decimal problems.

When I'd finally finished the math, I opened the Shaker book to begin reading. But I didn't open it to the place where I'd left off the night before; something made me open it at the beginning. At the pages before the beginning, actually. And there were the words: *To my parents, John and Margaret*

Tyler. I couldn't have written this without your love and support. S.T.

John and Margaret Tyler.

My grandparents! At last they had names!

I lifted my eyes from the book and looked over at Papa. He sat quietly, studying the newspaper, the way he did most nights. I got mad at him again, mad that he'd kept me from knowing my grandparents. Mad that he'd kept them from knowing about me.

I didn't sleep much that night. Ideas kept popping into my head. A trip. A trip to South Egremont, Massachusetts. By bus. I had money saved up, and Casey would lend me more if I needed it. Shoot, he might even go with me.

But what if they'd moved away from that town? What if they'd retired and gone to Florida?

So instead maybe I'd call them on the phone. Directory assistance would give me the number. There couldn't be too many John and Margaret Tylers in South Egremont, Massachusetts. I could call from Casey's house, so Papa wouldn't get a suspicious phone bill.

Ideas crowded my brain all night. When I got to school, I tried to tell Casey, but Ms. Custer made us say the pledge and get to work right away. I couldn't talk to him until lunch.

He popped open a can of juice. "Neat, Tyler. It's like a detective story. You have all these clues, and you're trying to trace the missing person."

"So can I use your phone? I have money saved. I'll pay for the call. I just don't want Papa to find out."

"Sure, Mom won't mind. Especially if it's for school. Geez, I'll pay for the call myself, just to see how it turns out. You want to try today?"

I nodded. "I'll ride over on my bike."

"There's one thing, though." Casey frowned. "Maybe you shouldn't just up and call. What if they think it's a prank call and hang up? Or start to cry? Or what if it's the wrong Tylers?"

Casey's words sent a chill up my spine. To work so hard to find my grandparents and then have them hang up the phone . . . I couldn't handle that. But what else could I do?

"Casey, I need to find out about my grandparents. Right away."

"Come on, Tyler, you haven't known them for eleven whole years. Give me five minutes to think."

My hands balled into fists for a moment. Then I opened my lunch bag and pulled out a peanut butter sandwich. I bit into it and chewed while Casey ripped open a bag of potato chips and set them on the table between us.

"The postmaster," he mumbled, his mouth partly full. He wiped his mouth with the back of his hand. "The post office is open Saturday mornings. What will you put in the letter? I mean, how do you go about telling somebody they've got a long-lost grandchild?"

I slurped down milk. "Casey, make sense. What's the point of talking to a postmaster in Ohio? My grandparents live in Massachusetts." I reached for a chip and crunched down hard, making as much noise as I could.

"Boy, are you thick, Tyler. Bet you stayed up all night worrying. You're only running on half your engines."

"Thanks a lot!" But he was right. I was tired.

"Look, I saw this detective show on TV. Here's what we do. We check the zip code book at the post office first thing. If there's a post office in South Eaglesmont—"

"South Egremont," I corrected.

"Whatever. We find their post office and send a letter to John and Margaret Tyler *inside* another letter, addressed to the postmaster. If you're real nice and ask him to mail the letter to the Tyler family whose daughter used to write those books—"

"They can't hang up on a letter," I interrupted. "And if they've moved, he can send the letter to Florida or wherever." Yes! Good old Casey.

"We'll use my address if you don't want your father to find out."

I frowned and stopped eating for a minute. "How can I get Papa to take me to the post office? It's too far to ride on my bike. I need some excuse."

My cheeks felt hot with shame. Lying to Papa and sneaking around in the attic . . . who was I turning into? But Papa had lied, too. He'd lied about me. About my whole life.

"We'll find your family, Ty," Casey said. "We'll call the post office after school today. We'll tell them it's a class project. They'll give us one puny little zip code over the phone." Casey munched a handful of chips and scribbled notes on the back of his lunch bag.

I watched his pencil scratch across that wrinkled brown paper and felt glad Casey Powell was on my side.

Chapter 15

I chewed on the end of my pen and read over the letter.

Dear Mr. and Mrs. Tyler,

You don't know about me, and I hope it's not too much of a shock. If you are the parents of Sarah Tyler who wrote books and married an Amish man named Jakob Stoudt, I'm your granddaughter. The doctors rushed in to save me, so I was born about half an hour after Mama's car was hit by the truck. They sent me to a baby hospital in Cleveland until I was strong enough to come home. Papa didn't tell you about me when you came for the funeral because he was afraid you'd take me away from him. After losing Mama, he couldn't chance that.

If you are my grandparents, maybe you can write me a letter and tell me about the family. I'm doing a family tree for school, and I need to know all the old stuff. But I'd really like to know more about you, too. Is there a picture you can send?

I'm sending you a copy of my school picture. It's last year's because this year's wasn't taken yet. I'm a little taller, but I look pretty much the same. I like to read books, and I'm good in science. I spend a lot of time in our woods, and I know about trees and birds and animals because I'm always out watching them.

Sincerely,
Your granddaughter (I hope),
Tyler Stoudt

"What do you think?"

I passed Casey the letter and chewed on my bottom lip as I waited for his reply. I had to put that part in about Papa. Sure, I was still mad at him, but I couldn't let those grandparents think he was heartless.

I wondered about signing it *Sincerely*. I was sincere. I meant every word in the letter. But did it sound too formal? I couldn't write *Yours truly,* because I didn't know if I was truly theirs or not. And I couldn't write *Love* because I didn't even know these people. How could I love them?

"They'll be more impressed if I copy it over," Casey offered.

"I'm not trying to impress them. I'm just trying to tell them who I am," I said. "My regular self."

"Okay, Ty," he said. "What do we put in the letter to the postmaster?"

It took a while, but between Casey and me, we finally wrote out everything we needed and stuffed it into the envelope. We put in extra stamps in case the Tylers had moved and the postmaster didn't know where. We used Casey's address for the return envelope, but I put mine inside the letter too, so they'd know Papa and I still lived in our own house and that Papa hadn't done something weird, like marrying Casey's mom. Most important, we put in the letter to John and Margaret Tyler.

I raised the flap to lick the glue on the envelope but stopped with the envelope in midair and my tongue sticking out. Slowly I lowered the envelope and dumped out all the papers inside.

Casey looked at me funny. "What's the matter, Ty? Change your mind?"

I shook my head. "No. I'll mail this letter, just like we planned. But can you think of a single reason why I shouldn't send another letter to Pennsylvania? To the Amish grandparents?"

Casey blinked a couple of times; he was thinking it over.

"I have cousins and aunts and uncles—fifteen years' worth. I know nothing about them," I explained. "If I have to build a family tree, I need all the branches. I even know the road where the Stoudts live. It's in Mama's book."

Casey looked at me, a million questions jumping from his eyes. He asked only one. The one that really mattered. "What will your father do?" he whispered. "What will he do if he finds out you wrote to his family?"

My voice felt shaky, and I took a deep breath. "He won't find out, Case. You and I are the only ones who know. And we're not telling. Please . . . don't make me stop. It's important . . . and hard already."

I stuck a piece of paper in his hands. "Please, Case," I said. "Please make a copy of the letter to the postmaster. We've got to finish before Papa comes in for lunch."

"You really want to do this, Tyler? Maybe you should think it over. Have enough stamps?"

I nodded slowly. I reached for my pen and started another letter, this time for the Stoudts.

Chapter 16

Once I sent off those two letters, I tried to stop worrying. There was nothing to do but wait. Wait for the postmasters to figure out where to send them. Then wait again to see if somebody wrote back.

The waiting was hard, but I had Mama's writings to think about. And Ms. Custer piled on plenty of work at school, too. So the Stoudts and the Tylers hovered there, in the back of my mind, like shadows waiting to come to life.

Mama was coming to life for me, though. She sat right up there in the front of my brain, telling me everything she thought. That afternoon, after Casey rode back home, I sneaked up to the attic again. This time I went prepared.

According to Papa, I was a trash collector. He was always after me to clean out my room and throw stuff away. I did the best I could. Every year at the end of school I went through my desk and threw away old papers from a couple years back. Last spring I threw away all my third-grade junk. I kept the fourth- and fifth-grade stuff, though. You never know when you'll need something.

That turned out to be a smart move. I took the fourth-grade papers up to the attic with me and stuck some in the box where I'd found Mama's handwritten notes. That way if Papa went up there, he wouldn't see any empty boxes.

I looked around again. I found three more big boxes of papers. When I opened the first one, I recognized the first page right off, the Shaker book. I'd just finished reading it. The box held Mama's handwritten copy of the book and some typed-up pages with scribbles in the margins. I hurried to check the other boxes, and sure enough, they were filled with the manuscripts of her two other published books. But I wanted something new to read. Something I hadn't seen before.

My fingers brushed a box thick with dust. Inside I found a tan folder. This wasn't just a new idea, like the ones I'd read the day before. The folder was fat—so Mama had spent plenty of time on these pages. I pulled it out and opened it carefully.

His name jumped out at me. *Jakob Stoudt.*

It was the book Mama had written about Papa. I emptied the box and refilled it with my fourth-grade math and science papers. Then I sneaked it back down to my room.

I wiped my hands on my jeans so I wouldn't get Mama's papers dirty and opened the folder again. *Jakob Stoudt.* Papa's name stood alone on the first page, no other title. That didn't make sense. She'd lived years after writing this book. She'd had time to think up a title. And shoot, she'd had plenty of time to turn this into a book. Why hadn't she?

I turned to the first page of text and began to read.

> *When Jakob hefts a board, his large hands weigh it; he sights down its length for signs of warp; he runs his callused thumb over its surface to read the grain. He chooses his wood with the care of an artist. Each board must be straight and cut true to the grain. And each board must align itself well with its neighbor. The sense of unity and harmony that so pervades an Amish commu-*

*nity is apparent in this plain man's workshop.
There is no dichotomy here, no distinction between life and work. Every aspect of this man's
life is given the respect it deserves, for it is a gift
from God.*

I looked up from the pages and swallowed hard.
To my eye, Mama's love for Papa showed in every
word. No wonder he missed her so much.

I read on as the afternoon turned from bright to
shadowed. I read how Papa had apprenticed himself to his uncle, Joseph Yoder, to learn cabinet-
making. He'd spent long hours mastering his
teacher's lessons and learned how to join boards
without screws or nails. He'd tried his own hand
at designing a piece of furniture. I watched,
through Mama's eyes, as he built a dish cupboard
for his sister Dorcas's new house.

I felt odd reading the pages. He was my papa.
I'd known him all my life. The things Mama
wrote about, I'd seen with my own eyes. And yet
in these pages he was different.

Supper felt strange that night. I peered at Papa
over my plate. I squinted at him as I cleared away
the dishes and brought baked apples for dessert.

"Do I have sawdust on my shirt, *liebchen*?" He

brushed his chest and smiled at me. "You look at me funny. Did I forget something when I washed up for supper?"

"No. It's my eyes. I was reading all afternoon. My eyes are tired." I told the truth, if not all the truth.

As I washed up the supper dishes I couldn't believe how dumb I'd been. For my whole life I'd taken Papa for granted, not imagining that he lived and worked by such different and wonderful beliefs. And I felt proud of my heritage. Proud that I came from strong people who knew what was really important.

Tired eyes or not, I needed to read more of Papa's story. How could I get to sleep unless I knew, in Mama's words, how the story ended?

So I stuck a towel on the floor by the door to block the light at the bottom, and I read late into the night. I read how Papa's business had flourished. How he'd set fair prices based on his costs and his time. How people had stood in line to buy his furniture because it was strong and because it was beautiful. When I got to the last page, I felt sad. I wanted to keep reading. I wanted to know more and more and more. But I came to the end and read Mama's last words.

Modern architects tell us that form is function, that beauty lies in utility. And some treat this dictum as a new and startling discovery. Meanwhile, in a wide valley south of Lancaster, Pennsylvania, a people live their whole lives by what they perceive as an ancient law. In plainness and simplicity, they seek the same truth. In his wood shop beside a pasture, Jakob Stoudt has surely found it.

"God made the trees," he says. "He has given me hands that understand the wood. How can I do less than my best with His gifts?"

I'd read all the way to the end of the book and still I wasn't satisfied. Because the end of the book was just the beginning of the story. And I wanted . . . no, I needed more.

Chapter 17

"Ladies. Gentlemen. Gather yourselves. Bring a notebook and a pencil. No purses or backpacks, please. They'll just get in the way."

"A field trip, Ms. Custer?" somebody asked. "How come our parents didn't sign slips?"

"We're taking a short walk," she said. "Just around the corner. But behave as if it's a field trip. Observe carefully and pay attention to the smallest details. They might prove important."

She smiled at us, and I saw a hint of something in her eyes. A surprise, maybe.

"Where do you think we're going?" I asked Casey. "There's nothing close to school." All the stores, the historical society, and the library were blocks away. An easy walk, but more than just around the corner.

Casey shrugged. "Wait and see," he said.

"Fine for you," I grumbled. "I'm waiting for too many things right now. I don't need surprises from Ms. Custer."

We shuffled out the front door and into a warm fall afternoon.

"I can't stand how she makes a big mystery out of a walk around the corner," Sissy Norman complained.

For once I agreed with Sissy. "She's treating us like babies. Remember when we were in kindergarten and we learned how to go for a walk?" I said. "We had to line up and grab a partner and walk in two little rows."

"Yeah. And I remember how you and Casey used to poke along at the end of the line and we always had to wait for you." Sissy shook her head. Then she grinned. "Do you and Casey want to be partners today? Hold hands?"

My face flamed. Sissy never could understand how Casey and I were friends. Just friends. She had to go and spoil things. I fumbled around for something to say, but as usual when Sissy put me on the spot, my brain stopped working.

"If we were partners, we'd be partners in

crime," Casey said in a deep, scary voice. "Tyler, let's find a garter snake or a toad to hide in French Fry's desk. Or a nest of mice for her locker."

"Disgusting!" Sissy sped up to walk ahead of us.

"Thanks," I said. "I think I'll stop trying to talk to her from now on."

Casey grinned. "Good idea."

"We're here," Ms. Custer announced.

Casey and I stood at the back of the line again, just like when we were little kids. I peered around to see where Ms. Custer had brought us. I couldn't figure it out. It was just a vacant lot.

"Divide yourselves up in groups of three or four. We'll study all the vegetation in the area." Ms. Custer assigned each group to a section of the lot and had us write down every single plant we saw. If we didn't know its name, somebody had to sketch the plant to look up later.

"This is one weird teacher," Michael Cohen said to Casey and me as we squatted on the ground. "She's making us draw weeds."

"Just be glad we've got Tyler," Casey said. "She knows the names of most of them."

"I have to yank them out of the garden," I grumbled. "Geez. There's so much stuff here."

"How about this? Where does it go on our list?" Michael held up a dented, faded beer can.

108

"Pitch it," I said. "Too far gone to recycle."

"Wait," Casey said. He grabbed the can. "You suppose somebody is living in there?" He poked at the side. "Hello. Anybody home?"

He put the can to his ear and listened. Then he squinted into the opening. "Little green men," he said. "They want us to take them to our leader. They also want us to take them to lunch."

"I wonder what they eat," I said. "Burgers and fries?"

"Fries! We could give them to French Fry," Casey said. He had a wicked grin on his face.

"How many plants do we need on our lists, Ms. Custer?" Sissy's voice carried across the lot, and the three of us giggled.

"All of them," our teacher replied. She smiled. Casey rolled his eyes at me.

"Last year's class warned us," I said.

"But we didn't know she was weird," Michael said. "Old Vanilla Pudding. Weirdest teacher in the world."

I went back to writing down plants. I didn't like the way kids called Ms. Custer *Vanilla Pudding*. She couldn't help having her last name.

Just like I couldn't help being a Tyler and a Stoudt.

Chapter 18

I didn't talk much as we walked back to school. Questions jiggled in my head, and I needed time to make sense of everything. Why had Ms. Custer dragged us to an empty lot to make a list of weeds? And why had she started that family tree business in the first place?

I kicked at a stone on the sidewalk. Sometimes I wished she'd never had the idea. Sometimes I wanted to thank her for opening up my family's secrets. But there were still secrets out there, secrets I needed to uncover.

When we got back to class, Ms. Custer started one of her famous lists on the blackboard. "First let's note the plants you found," she said. "And then think of some of the characteristics those plants have in common."

"They're green," Casey offered. He grinned and wriggled his eyebrows at me.

I grinned back.

We kept Ms. Custer busy writing out a long list of plants. After she copied the last one, she pointed to the other column on the board. "Characteristics, ladies and gentlemen. What were those plants like? So far I know only that they were green."

Casey grinned again, and I shook my head at him.

"Some are tough plants," I said. "Like crab-grass. It grows back no matter how many times you pull it out."

"Yeah," somebody in the back said. "My dad says dandelions are stubborn. They never die."

The second list grew: *Tough. Stubborn. Strong. Sturdy. Healthy. Hardy.*

"Anybody want to guess why we went to the vacant lot today?" Ms. Custer asked. "Two hints. First, look at the list of traits. And second, think about this. Those plants grow in an *empty* lot. In ecological terms, they're called colonizing plants."

A lightbulb switched on in my head. Other kids must have felt the same way, because people said aloud what I was thinking. "Our ancestors . . .

111

people who came here to settle . . . people in our family trees . . ."

I looked again at the list on the board. *Tough* and *stubborn. Strong. Sturdy. Healthy* and *hardy.* You'd have to be a human dandelion to cross an ocean and start life in a brand-new place.

Ms. Custer was some weird teacher all right. She threw curveballs. She made us do projects that seemed simple and easy, but there was always something hiding underneath. I liked it, though. Liked the way she got us thinking about things. I tuned in to the discussion boiling around me.

". . . the people who came here *for* something were more important . . . more than the ones who came here to escape."

"Important how?" Ms. Custer asked.

"Important in starting the country, I guess," Casey said. "My family came here to make a better life. To own land. And pass that land on to their kids."

"You're wrong, Casey," Sissy argued. "Sure, people came here to get rich. That's okay, I guess. But it's not as good."

"What do you think was good, Sissy?" Our teacher pushed for more ideas.

Sissy tried again. "Well . . . the ones who

came for religion. Or politics. They came for . . . for beliefs. Not just money."

From the looks on their faces, they'd been arguing for a while. Seemed like a dumb fight. "You're both right," I said, remembering about Casey's ancestors and the potato famine. "People who came to make a better life were also escaping. From being poor and hungry."

"And?" Ms. Custer prompted.

I couldn't think of anything else to say. I was glad when Mimi Deng finished my sentence for me.

"And making a better life for your kids is a belief, too. Like having your own religion."

"Yes," Michael Cohen said. "People came to America to escape bad stuff and find better stuff. Not one or the other. My family came for both."

Ms. Custer was an amazing teacher, all right. If I closed my eyes, I could almost hear our brains stretching inside our heads. Our whole class—even Sissy and Casey, for all their squabbling—was talking about real history, and it made sense.

"That's it. That's exactly it!" I said in a loud voice. "Everybody came here to find freedom. All our ancestors. Even the people who are coming here today."

"Are you sure about that?"

Her voice came from behind me and to the left. When I turned and saw who was talking, I swallowed hard. Jasmine Williams. The minute I saw her serious face, I knew we were all forgetting something. Something important.

The room grew still, and we waited for her to finish. We were ashamed of ourselves. At least I was. Because I knew what she was going to say. And she was right.

"My African ancestors didn't come here to find freedom," she said. "They were brought here. To be slaves. We're still fighting for freedom."

She spoke in a quiet but steady voice, and I admired the way she stood up to all our staring. Again, like the day Michael had told us about his grandparents escaping from Hitler's Germany, I wondered about all the people who had come before.

"Thank you, Jasmine," Ms. Custer said. "You remind us that we can't claim only the idealistic individuals in our history. African Americans and Native Americans have a somewhat different view, as we shall see as the year proceeds."

Thank you, Jasmine, I wanted to add, but I was too chicken to say it out loud. *Thanks for showing me I'm not the only one who's different.*

But compared to Jasmine, I had it easy. I could decide whether or not to tell people about my Amish family. Jasmine didn't have any choice. She wore her heritage every day.

If I ever got up the nerve to tell the truth, Jasmine might understand. But the thought of telling turned my insides to mush.

I'd never tell. I was a coward. Plain and simple.

Chapter 19

M s. Custer had loaded on the homework, pages of math and a big list of vocabulary words. I stopped to hug Papa in his shop and grab an apple from a bowl in the kitchen. Then I raced upstairs and dumped my books on my bed. I felt all charged up about my family's history, partly from class and partly from reading about Papa.

I needed to find the next chapters in the story of my parents falling in love and getting married. So I grabbed more old school papers and climbed the attic steps. I went through four boxes of mixed-up papers before I saw the stack of notebooks. I stared at those black-and-white speckled covers.

Open me! Read me! they seemed to shout. So I did.

Today is the first day of my real life. I have a job, an apartment, and a book to write. The job isn't much. Working in the Williams College library won't send me to Paris or Rome. But I don't need a lot of money. I just need enough to get by, so I can write . . .

Oh, Mama, I thought. *You were so young, and your life was just beginning. Why did it have to end so fast?*

I read a little more—about how she'd studied the Shakers in college and how some professor wanted her to try to turn her research into a book. Then I flipped pages.

If I'd been more patient, or less nosy, I'd have gone through the notebooks from beginning to end. I'd have read Mama's everyday thoughts in order. I wanted to do that. To meet this young, sweet mama of mine and watch her live her life. But I hated waiting. So I flipped pages, looking at dates and watching for the first mention of the Amish.

I found it partway into the third book. Mama had gone through a notebook a year, so she'd been about twenty-five by the time she found Papa. She still lived in Massachusetts, still worked at that college library. But they didn't need her in the summers, so when June came she went off to find out about an Amish wedding.

. . . strange customs here. The young men do all the courting, and it's always in secret. The young women must pretend total uninterest. From the looks on their faces, I'd say the pretense doesn't fool too many people. The young men receive courting buggies at about sixteen—the same age we English get our driver's licenses. Heavens, listen to me. I've been here two days and I'm already sounding like a member of the community. We English indeed . . .

Interesting stuff. Stuff she hadn't put in her book. Her personal, private opinions. But I'd read about this part of her life already. So I skimmed. I hurried through until the sight of Papa's name caught my eye. No, that sentence didn't matter. Mama had just mentioned him as Dorcas Stoudt's brother.

I scanned the pages again, watching the dates. Mama was finishing her book on Aunt Dorcas. She had enough material so that she could go home and finish writing.

Dorcas was married today, and I was privileged to attend the ceremony. Her brother Jakob explained to me in advance all the parts of the service, so although I didn't understand the archaic German, I could sense what was happening and when. There was a soft light in his eyes when he told of the wedding, and I had to force myself to look away. Weddings do strange things to people. I am a romantic fool, making something of nothing.

My hands tightened on the notebook as I read on.

I have become so accustomed to seeing the women in plain clothing, it seems completely natural that Dorcas should be married in a dress that she will wear again tomorrow and next week. A dress that she will cook in and garden in and tend her babies in someday.

Time to leave Lancaster. I have more than used up my welcome with these lovely people. Yet something tugs at me. I can't identify exactly what. Perhaps it is the simplicity of their lifestyle. Or the rich beauty of the land.

No. This isn't a manuscript. This is where I

tell the truth. The whole truth. To myself. I'll admit it. I feel drawn to these people and particularly to Jakob Stoudt. The man isn't exceptionally handsome or outlandishly charming. But there is something about him. His roots reach down into the past, solid and strong. And yet in spite of . . . No. Because of his strength, he is probably the gentlest man I've ever known. What a change from Roger and his cleft chin and his superior attitudes.

Strange. I've never even seen Jakob alone, but a spark flies between us. I feel it every time he catches my eye. Surely his family must notice. Nothing gets by that Reuben.

I must leave. For Jakob's safety and for my own.

Who was Roger? Some dumb old stuck-up boyfriend, I bet. I could barely imagine Mama herself, let alone think about her having boyfriends before she met Papa.

Reading this felt like listening in when nobody knew you were around. Once in fifth grade I'd taken the attendance list to the school office and overheard two teachers discussing their boyfriends. For at least a month after, my ears turned red every time I saw those teachers.

I was intruding.

But wait, this was Mama and Papa. I had to know what had happened with them.

I closed my eyes and promised myself not to read anything I wouldn't want my someday daughter reading about me.

I looked out the window. The sun hung low in the sky. I gathered up all Mama's notebooks and refilled the boxes with fifth-grade junk. I headed downstairs. At least in my room, I could pretend I was working on homework.

I read on. Read how Mama had gone to work on the book back at home in Massachusetts. Her publisher had liked it and sent her a check. She'd decided to take some time off and write about Papa.

It seems like too much of a coincidence. The Shaker and Mormon books are selling well. My savings and the advance on the book about the Amish wedding would keep me going for at least six months, even without the other royalties. It's time to wing it. Time to quit the routine job and plunge into the writing.

But I can't get Jakob Stoudt out of my mind. The more I try to push him away, the more I see his face, smiling at me across his mother's supper

table. I'm meant to go back to Lancaster. To go
back and write about Jakob and get him out of my
system for good. Haven't I already written a chap-
ter and an outline without a single interview?

This can't be a coincidence. I have enough
money to live on and a book that's practically
writing itself. What kind of writer will I be if I
let the possibility that I may be hurt get in the
way? No. I'll go to Lancaster with an open heart.
If Jakob will let me write about him . . .

Mama had gone back to Lancaster and spent a
lot of time with Papa. I could tell that she'd loved
him, even though I'd never fallen in love in my
life and didn't know the symptoms.

Mama had tried to pretend it was just the book
she was writing. I laughed when I read that part.
How she'd always gotten fascinated by the people
she wrote about, and since she'd never written
about a man before, the fascination was a bit
stronger.

I read her notebook until I got to the place
where she'd finished the book about Papa. And
then I read a little further.

I thought . . . no, hoped *I would get over*
this infatuation with Jakob. I was kidding myself.

As he checks for rough spots on the arm of a chair, I want it to be my arm he's touching. So I've finished the book and I've fallen in love with this man. And yet, even now, I know that if I truly love him, I'll pack my suitcases and leave town for good. For my love is the very thing that will destroy him.

I love him for his simple, plain ways. For the unaffected gentleness that spills out of every word, every gesture. And yet if I show this love, if I go to Jakob, his way of life will be finished. He will lose the connection to his people and his land that makes him so strong. So I'm packing. Tonight I'll pack, and tomorrow I'll say my goodbyes. . . .

No, Mama. You can't leave. You cannot leave Lancaster without Papa. And of course she hadn't.

Jakob will not accept goodbye. He took me in his arms and held me close. I have never felt so cherished in my entire life.

He wants me to marry him. I don't know whether to laugh or cry. Of course I'm overjoyed that he returns my love. I feel like a giddy teen-ager again. But I hate the consequences. Jakob's family is conservative, even among the Amish. Old Order, they call it. They will shun him if he marries me. He will become an orphan overnight. Is one woman's love strong enough to replace an entire community?

I argued with him. Told him he'd get over me. He put his finger on my lips to stop my words. He said we were meant to find each other. Why else had I come back to write his story? Why had he remained unmarried when many Amish marry before they turn twenty? Why had I earned enough money to live for a while without my library job? Why had he learned to work with wood, a movable skill?

I gave in then, stopped arguing.

It's three days later. Today we were married by a minister in Lancaster. Not by an Amish minister, though. To the Amish we were already dead and buried. Verboten! *So my Jakob and I were married on our way out of town.*

I let the notebook drop into my lap. I couldn't read another word for a while. The sweetness of Mama and Papa's story made me happy and sad together. But the way his family had treated them left a sour taste in my mouth.

Sweet. Sour. I'd heard that before. No, read it, right there in Mama's notebook. She'd written about a supper with the whole Stoudt family. My grandmother Rachel had served seven sweets and seven sours at the meal.

Seven sweets and seven sours. They thought it made for a balanced meal. Maybe they thought sourness was good in your life, too. Well, too bad for them. They'd turned so sour toward Papa they'd missed out on knowing Mama and me.

I hid Mama's notebooks under my bed and wandered downstairs to fix our own supper. I defrosted some ground meat so I could make hamburgers and salad, the most un-Amish meal I could think of.

Then I poked around in the cupboard and found a brownie mix. Papa didn't usually buy stuff like that, but I was glad he'd gotten this one. Because I wanted something sweet. Totally and completely sweet. No sours at all.

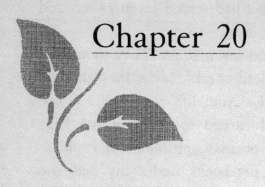

Chapter 20

My mouth took a couple of days to lose the sour taste. If I hadn't already mailed my letter to Lancaster, I'd have ripped it up, I was so mad at those Amish grandparents. By the time I read the next part of Mama's notebook, I wanted to tear up the letter to the Tylers, too. Her parents were just as stubborn and mean as the Stoudts.

Jakob and I spent several days traveling about. He is amazed by the things I take for granted. He says he won't mind electricity and indoor plumbing but can't understand why the English spend so much time watching TV. I'm not sure if it's the photographic images that offend him or the mindless content of the shows. In any case, I'll sell my television. I've also agreed to teach him to drive a car, but the thought makes me nervous. For a gentle man, he drove his buggy as fast as his horse would run.

We spent a week ambling back to Massachusetts. We unloaded Jakob's tools and his belongings, but my apartment is crowded. We need a place with room for a shop. Maybe an old farmhouse. But first, my parents. I should call ahead and tell them about getting married, but I'm tempted to just drive down and surprise them. . . .

Sometimes I'm the stupidest woman alive. Whatever made me think my parents would be open-minded or understanding? First they thought Jakob was some long-haired hippie. Dad took off on his anti-Communist speech. When I told them Jakob was more conservative than they were, that he was Amish, Dad exploded. Called me a soft-hearted fool. Called Jakob a simple peasant. I sensed that Mom wanted to like him, but she'd never openly defy Dad. We fought for two days.

So now we are two orphans. We need to put

distance between us and our families. Dear God, it hurts. I thought I understood what Jakob gave up when he married me, but I'm only now feeling it for real. I've been shunned, too. Of course, we English are too civilized to call it shunning. But whatever name you use, it hurts to be cut off.

I knew all this stuff. Papa had told me. But it hurt all the same to read it in Mama's words. My temper simmered away.

I read on for a while as Mama and Papa gathered their belongings and prepared to move. Mama had a friend who lived in northern Ohio and knew about a small farm for sale. It wasn't right in the middle of an Ohio Amish community, but it wasn't far, either.

The rolling land reminded Papa of his home. So they bought our house and fixed it up. Mama took part-time jobs and wrote stories for a couple of local newspapers and magazines. She worked for the nearby college, too. Papa set up his shop and built furniture for our house, samples he could use to show customers.

Mostly Mama's notebook made it sound like they were pioneers, moving west and starting up a new life. Only once in a while did she get mad. In one of the mad parts, I finally found out why the book about Papa still sat in a box.

A grim, rainy February day. I spent the morning helping Jakob repair a gap in the kitchen wall that lets in cold air. We had fun working together. Reminds me of the days I spent watching him in his shop in Lancaster County. But remembering still hurts.

I haven't been able to send off the manuscript. My reluctance comes from many sources—I must sort it out and decide what to do.

I'm still angry with his family and the Amish in general. I don't want to publish another book about them. I could get over that. Especially if I went back and edited it so the book focused on Jakob and his particular story. Honestly, sometimes he amazes me. As often as I'm mad at his family, I have to bless them for making him the man he is. Jakob has such a strong spirit, such a deep and faithful soul, that he endures this banishment with courage and grace. So perhaps I should go ahead and send the book. . . .

But there's more. The Jakob I wrote about doesn't exist now. He isn't a part of the Amish community. In writing the book I altered the re-

ality I encountered. Do I let the book stand as a historical document? Do I change the ending to show what really happened? Do I rewrite the entire thing as an improbable love story?

If I do send it off, my instincts say to send it as is. But then what? Jakob copes so well with the upheavals in his life, but will reading the book cause him pain? Regrets? I love him too much to inflict additional hurt. Heaven knows I've done enough of that.

I had a funny feeling about that book. Nowhere had Mama mentioned talking the book over with Papa. What if he'd never seen it? I bet he hadn't looked at a single notebook, either. He must have missed Mama so much at first that I bet he'd just packed everything away, saving the stuff in the trunk for me. Maybe he'd wondered why she never published the book about him. I'd have wondered. I'd have felt hurt.

I read on in the notebooks. Pages about the farm and the jobs Mama had. Papa's business grew, so they were doing all right. When I came to the part about me, I had to steady my hands. They shook so badly that at first I couldn't read a single word.

Our prayers have been answered. A child is on the way. Jakob had tears in his eyes when I told him. I hope that in some way this new life will make up to him for those he left behind.

He is building a cradle. I sit with him in the shop while he smooths the boards and we talk about our child. Perhaps we are too idealistic, but I hope not. We want to bring this baby up with the best of our two backgrounds—the faith, humility, and gentleness of spirit that Jakob learned among the Amish. The curiosity and thirst for learning that I have known all my life. And we have agreed that the baby will learn to include others, not exclude them. To accept differences rather than fear them.

When I carry on about this for too long, Jakob smiles at me and says that building the cradle is the easy part. Building the life will be hard work. But I take it on willingly. Yes. I embrace it.

My eyes puddled up on me.

I'd always felt loved. Never once had I thought Papa didn't care for me with his whole heart. But here I saw Mama's side of things. Mama had loved me, too, even if she hadn't lived long enough to show me. Somehow her words healed a sore place inside, a place that had hurt ever since I'd found out she died.

I hugged her notebook to me, proof of that love. And I wondered, just for a moment, if reading the notebooks might heal Papa, too.

Chapter 21

As I read Mama's notebooks I soaked up the past like an old towel soaks up a spill. I hardly paid attention to the present. Dumb of me, really dumb.

It started out as an ordinary Friday in October. Indian-summer weather. We had a math test, and I did okay. Even Casey didn't panic for once. Busy playing detective for me, he forgot to get nervous about the test. If the good weather held, he and I would scout the woods for walnuts and hickory nuts before squirrels stole them all.

I climbed off the school bus, planning to get every speck of homework done so I'd have Saturday and Sunday free. When I walked up the driveway toward the house, I saw it. An Amish buggy had pulled up to the front porch.

I knew without a second's thought that my letter had brought that buggy—the buggy and the man who climbed down from the seat as I watched.

Somehow I unfroze my muscles and hurried toward the house.

The man seemed to know to head toward the barn at this time of day. He called out in a loud voice. "Jakob? Jakob Stoudt?"

I got to Papa's shop just as the door opened. Papa poked his head out and said, "*Ja*. I'm Jakob Stoudt." Then he stopped. His eyes shone, and tears spilled out on his cheeks. "Levi? Dear *Gott*, is that you, Levi?"

Papa hugged the man, and they were both talking in German, so fast I couldn't keep up. I made out the words *how* and *why* as Papa said them.

Then the man, the man who had to be my uncle Levi, reached into his pocket. He reached into his pocket and pulled out an envelope. My letter.

I had to explain. I opened my mouth to try, but the words stuck in the back of my throat.

Papa reached for the letter.

I swallowed hard and dug deep for courage. "I did it, Papa. I wrote to them."

Both men turned to stare at me like I'd just landed in a spaceship from Mars.

In a way, I had. Talking in German, Papa had sounded like he'd gone back to his Amish self. Now I'd reminded him of who he really was. He took a step away from his brother.

"We better go inside and sit down," Papa said. He spoke English, but slowly, like he thought about each word before it came out. "Levi, my daughter, Tyler. Tyler, meet Levi Stoudt."

I tried to smile. "H-Hello," I stammered. "Hello, Uncle Levi."

"Plain Levi is fine with me," he said with a smile. "We don't think much of titles." He took my hand in his and half squeezed, half shook it.

I studied his face as we walked toward the back door. Even if I didn't know his name, surely I'd have guessed he was Papa's brother. Underneath his wide hat brim, his brown hair grew thick like Papa's. And his eyes. He had Papa's dark brown eyes, which crinkled up at the corners when he smiled.

"You and I will speak later," Papa whispered to me as he held open the door. "Can you pour some cider for my brother?"

I nodded, hearing the stern tone in Papa's voice. I hurried to the kitchen. They followed.

They spoke mostly English with just a little German thrown in.

"Your life goes well, brother?" Levi asked Papa.

"*Ja*. And yours?"

Levi nodded. "I understand from the letter that your wife has died, Jakob. I am sorry."

"*Danke.*"

I wished Papa would ask about the rest of the family, but he didn't. "Why did you come?" he asked. "Have the people changed? Am I not shunned?"

"*Ja*. You are still under the ban."

"Then how can you come? It's a long way. Don't you put yourself in trouble?"

I poured cider into three glasses and passed them around. My fingers held the glasses so tightly, I was afraid they'd shatter. I slid into a chair at the end of the table and listened.

"My wife has family in Ohio, so we come on the train to see them. A young cousin loaned me his buggy."

"But the shunning?" Papa spoke low. Painful words.

Levi looked just as serious. "I spoke with the bishop, Jakob. He blessed my trip. You know it is not a sin to speak with a person under the ban if it is your devout hope to bring that person back to *Gott*."

"I do not believe that *Gott* has left me behind," Papa said in a firm voice.

His temper was heating up. I couldn't blame him. First he'd found out about my sending that letter. Now his brother was accusing him.

"Jakob. Hear me out. I am come here to speak with you. If your heart is willing, you could come back to Lancaster with me. You could repent now that you are no longer married to an English."

"I? I could repent of my life? Of my wife and my child? Look at her, Levi." He pointed to me.

My face burned. I stared at the floor and tugged at the tail of my shirt.

"Look at her face and tell me she is a sin. No! I am who I am. There is no going back."

Levi grinned and raised his glass to Papa. "I know, Jakob. In my heart I guessed you would say no. You were always a stubborn man. But as long as I am come for your soul, I have come in good faith, *ja?* And now that I am here, should I turn back to Pennsylvania? Or should I stay awhile and drink this good cider and see if maybe you change your mind?"

Papa laughed then. He crossed the room to sit

next to Levi and slapped his brother on the shoulder. "You always could get your own way, little brother. Tell me, how are Reuben and Joseph and the girls?"

Papa and Levi changed moods too fast for me. As they talked on, I figured it out. Levi had come to try to bring Papa back to his faith. But he also wanted to see his brother again.

Levi told about his wife and children, about each brother and sister. He told about all the cousins. He told about the grandparents, Titus and Rachel. How they were growing old and had turned the farm over to Reuben and Joseph.

At some point during the long conversation I managed to fix supper. I might as well have cooked cardboard, for all the notice we took of the food.

Papa and Levi ate theirs without complaining, and mine disappeared from my plate. But I couldn't taste whether I was eating ham or hamburger. My mouth was too busy biting back the hundreds of questions I wanted to ask but couldn't.

And I worried, too. What would Papa do when Levi left us?

Chapter 22

Levi and Papa talked into the night. I sat up as long as I could, but Papa sent me to bed when my eyes wouldn't stay open anymore. After breakfast the next morning, he asked me to show Levi our woods. At last I had time to ask all my questions.

Once I had my uncle to myself, I hardly knew where to begin. I mostly wanted to shout at him for shunning Papa. But how could I do that? If I yelled, Levi would tell Papa, and Papa would be shamed.

"You like the woods, Tyler? My brother says you know all the trees."

I nodded. Levi had just given me my beginning.

"I do. I know about maples and oaks and all

kinds of evergreens. But I don't know much about my family tree."

Levi looked at me with a wrinkled-up face, and I realized he didn't understand about family trees.

"My relatives," I went on. "I liked when you told about all my cousins last night. But I don't know what they look like. Do you have pictures?"

He shook his head and ducked under a low hanging branch. "No. We do not allow photographs."

I felt dumb. I knew they didn't take pictures. From my mother's writing, I'd found out lots of things about how the Stoudt family lived. But I didn't know why. With Levi there, I could ask.

"Are pictures too modern?"

"Partly they're modern. But more. We see them as unholy. The Bible tells us not to make images."

Unholy? Papa liked a simple, plain life, but he didn't call modern things unholy.

"And you could come to Lancaster to see what your cousins look like." He smiled at me.

What? That sounded like an invitation to visit. I kicked at a pile of yellow leaves.

"Come to Lancaster? How?"

"There is a train."

"No. I mean, how could I come and see my cousins? Papa is still shunned, isn't he?"

"*Ja.* He is shunned. But you, Tyler, you can come."

"No. I'm shunned, too. I won't visit any place Papa isn't welcome."

"We don't shun children. But *ja,* I understand."

I lost it then. I totally and completely lost my temper. I spun around and glared up into my uncle's face.

"Well, I don't. I don't understand it a bit. How can you just pretend Papa is dead? That's more unholy than taking photographs. My papa hasn't lost his God. And he's still a good man. The best!"

"*Ja,* Tyler. You are angry. I understand that, too. Maybe we can sit down and talk. Is there a clearing nearby?"

I stomped through the underbrush to a meadow. I flopped to the ground and scowled up at him. Him in his baggy old-fashioned pants and his black hat. And that beard. I couldn't see much of his face between the hat and the beard, so I had no idea what he was thinking.

He sat beside me, pulled up a blade of grass, and stuck it in his mouth.

"If you're so good at understanding, how come you're still shunning Papa?" I demanded.

"Let me tell you a story, Tyler. A true story.

Then maybe you will understand me as well as I understand you."

Fat chance of that. I shredded a maple leaf into tiny flakes.

"Once there was a boy. A plain boy. He had seven brothers and sisters, all of them good and worthy people. But one brother was the boy's favorite. The second oldest. He carried the boy on his shoulders. He taught the boy to fill the woodbox and surprise their papa. He showed the boy how to carve sticks with a knife, and he let him help in the wood shop."

I could tell already that Levi was the boy and Papa the big brother. Levi's words came right out of my childhood. Papa had done those things with me, too. It made a connection between Levi and me, a bridge.

Levi patted my hand and went on. "The boy was twelve when the brother left. And the boy missed his big brother. He didn't understand why Mama and Papa grew so angry. He didn't understand why all the others would not speak the brother's name. Or why his wood shop was taken down. *Ja,* Tyler. I am that boy. Jakob is the brother."

"You loved him. How could you let it happen?"

"I still love him. I was a child then. I argued and argued, but I couldn't stop the shunning. Now I am a man. Now I understand the reasons."

I shook my head. "No. There are no reasons for shunning."

Levi continued as if I hadn't interrupted. "We Amish are a strong people. We believe in *Gott* and the Bible. We try to live a life of simple holiness. And when we're not sure what to do, we read the Bible again to find out."

"But the Bible doesn't say shun your brother! It says love him."

"*Ja.* The shunning is the hard part of the loving. For us, the life is strict. If we become modern, we lose our faith, our ways."

"So if someone does something that is modern . . ."

"He must stop. Or leave. Our ways go back a long time. But if we change, even a little bit, then we will change a little more and then more, until we are just like the English. And then we will lose our *Gott.*"

I tried to understand. Best I could figure, it was like training for the Olympics. You worked hard until your body got sore. You couldn't let up, not for a second, if you wanted to win. You could only relax when the race was over. For the Amish, life was always hard. For them, the race was never over; they never relaxed their rules.

"So when Papa married Mama," I asked, "he couldn't stay a real Amish man?"

"Not quite. If your mother took on our ways, we would accept Jakob back. But he was proud. He would not ask her. He loved her as she was. And he knew our ways. Before he married her, he knew he would have to leave."

I tried hard to understand, but the thought of them kicking Papa out of the family felt sour. It still hurt. I told Levi so.

"*Ja*. It hurts me, too. Fifteen years and it hurts. Sometimes you make a sacrifice for what you believe, even if it hurts you for your whole life."

Chapter 23

After our walk, Levi hitched the horse to the borrowed buggy. He went inside to get his clothes.

I stroked the forehead of the brown horse. Then I climbed into the buggy. The seat felt stiff, worse than the seat in Papa's old truck. It made me think again about how hard the Amish life must be.

Levi helped me down from the buggy. He took my hand and told me to take care of Papa. I said I would. He also gave me a folded piece of paper.

"Your cousins' names," he explained.

Then he and Papa said goodbye.

"Will you think about it, Jakob? Just think a little about it."

Papa shook his head. "And you say I'm the

stubborn one, brother." He laughed. "Look at me. I button my shirt. I zipper my jacket. I have electric lights and indoor bathrooms. No, Levi. I am not Amish anymore."

"Are you English, then? Do you spend your time piling up money so you can show off to your neighbors? Is your house full of fancy decorations?"

Levi's words caught me by surprise. The Amish saw the English as showing-off people. That's why they wanted to keep us from spoiling their ways. I didn't feel like a spoiler.

A sadness washed over Papa's face. "No, Levi. I am not English, either. Not Amish, not English. I guess I am not anything."

You are something, I wanted to shout. *You are my father!* I bit back the words.

Levi threw his arm around Papa's shoulders. "I will come back, Jakob. Saving souls can take many visits. I will come again next fall to see if you wish to change your mind."

"You waste your trip," Papa protested.

"Maybe," replied Levi. "I leave that in the hands of *Gott.* Stay well, brother."

He climbed into the borrowed buggy and waved before turning down the drive toward the road.

I stood next to Papa and watched dust kick up as my uncle left us. Papa put his arm around my shoulder, and we didn't speak until the buggy disappeared around a curve in the road.

"Well, Tyler. A surprising two days. Tell me about this letter of yours."

I was in for it now. I sat down on the front step.

"I'm sorry, Papa. I didn't mean to cause trouble. I just wanted to find out about my cousins." I unfolded the paper in my hands and looked at all the old-fashioned names.

"This is not a thing to be sorry for," he said. He sat down beside me and hugged me tightly. "Doing this in secret, not telling—that was wrong. But your letter brought something good. It gave me a brother back. And he will come again. I know Levi. He was an independent boy. He is an independent man. He will come for my soul, and for a visit."

"I like him. He reminds me of you, Papa. But I'm still mad about the shunning."

"*Ja*. Your mother felt the same way. I accept because I know the people's ways. Your mother was angry."

My mother! If I'd been brave then, I'd have told about the other letter, the Tyler one. And my trips to the attic. But I wasn't brave.

A long time had passed since I mailed the Massachusetts letter. No answer. Either the postmaster was too busy or my grandparents weren't interested in me. I didn't want to upset Papa any more. So I said nothing.

While I waited for Casey to arrive, I got out cloth bags to gather walnuts and hickory nuts. I thought about Uncle Levi and about all the Stoudts. But mostly I thought about Papa.

I am not English. Not Amish, not English. I guess I am not anything.

Those words upset me. I wanted to make Papa feel better. To make him feel like something again. I thought hard, but my mind came up blank.

"Hey, Tyler," Casey called as he rode up the drive. He climbed off his bike and leaned it against the porch. "Sorry I'm late. Mom made me cut the grass first. Took forever. Hope you didn't start without me."

"Nope. But you missed something. Some*body*. My uncle Levi came to see us. My *Amish* uncle Levi."

"Wow! So the letter worked! What was he like? Did he have one of those big hats on? Did he have a horse and buggy? Was your father mad about the letter?"

I told Casey about Levi's visit as we walked into the woods. I only left out one part, about Papa feeling like he wasn't anything. That seemed too private.

Still, I had a lot to tell, and we each filled a bag with nuts before I finished. I showed him the list with all the cousins.

"Amazing. Your family tree has a zillion branches." He counted up all my new cousins. "Bet your uncle gave you more stuff to write about for that report, too."

"I suppose so."

I'd written my report already. Finished it! I'd written about Germany and religious freedom in general. But I hadn't mentioned any dates or the word *Amish*.

I let my fingers slide over the bumps on a walnut shell. Papa's words came back to me again: *I am not anything*.

What would he think if I left out the Amish part of my family history? Would he think I was ashamed of his early life? Of him?

Would he be right?

Chapter 24

All weekend I worried. Tuesday it would be my turn to read the dumb report to the class. I was tempted to ask Ms. Custer if I could get out of it, but that would mean telling her I was ashamed of Papa and his family. Even if I felt that way a little, I didn't want to admit it out loud. Ms. Custer had been nice to me. She seemed to think I was a good student, a good person. I couldn't risk changing her mind. But what would the kids say?

Monday night I flopped around in bed trying to get comfortable. Nothing worked. So I crept to the bathroom, grabbed a towel, and stuck it under the door to my room. I turned on the light and pulled out Mama's journal and the book about Papa's family.

"Please, Mama," I whispered. "I'm so mixed up. Please tell me what to do."

I read for a while in the journal. With every word, I felt Mama tugging at my mind. She'd been so in love with Papa, so proud of him. How dare I keep his past a secret?

But he'd kept it a secret, hadn't he? He'd lied to me and about me. If I lied about him, I'd just be paying him back.

I opened the Amish book, the published one, and flipped through it. Just in case I wanted to change my report, I needed to know the exact facts. When and why had the Amish come to Pennsylvania in the first place? Which towns had they come from? I'd read it once, but then I'd been more interested in finding my family tree. Now I wanted to understand why it had been transplanted.

I sighed. Maybe what I should do was write two reports, one with and one without the Amish part. Then the next day I could decide which one to read. Sure, I'd be putting it off, but so what?

I found the right chapter and studied it like a big test was coming up. The dates, the names of the Amish leaders, it was all there. But there was more. There was Mama's opinion about it. I could hardly breathe when I read that part.

. . . and so a plain and God-fearing people risked their lives to cross an ocean, to find a land where they could obey God's laws. The Amish were not a proud people, not showy, but they held their heads high and proclaimed what they believed.

And in their new country, generation after generation, they continue to risk the scorn of their neighbors, the ridicule of the worldly, as they live out their lives in simple obedience. These are the Stoudts of Lancaster County, Pennsylvania.

I swallowed hard. I'd asked Mama what to do, and in her own way she'd told me. Now it was up to me. I had to be strong enough to do as she'd suggested. I got out my paper and pencil.

My knees felt weak the next morning when I climbed the steps to school.

"Tyler! Guess what!"

"Later, Casey. I'm nervous about my report."

"But Tyler—"

"Later, Casey. I'm a wreck."

I raced to the classroom and found Ms. Custer sorting the corrected spelling tests from the week before. "About my report . . . please, can I go first?"

"Yes, Tyler, you may be first. We'll start right after the pledge."

Never had it taken such a short time for our class to find seats, get quiet, and recite the pledge to the flag. I mouthed the words and held my hand over my heart. It thumped so hard I was sure I'd bruise my chest.

Ms. Custer nodded to me, and I walked to the front of the room. I took a deep breath and clutched the pages of my report with damp hands. I squinted at the words and wished I'd written twice as large.

"Go, Tyler," Casey whispered.

I looked at him, and he grinned. He stuck both thumbs in the air, giving me the courage to start reading. And once I started, I didn't even need the papers or the words. I knew this stuff by heart. It was, after all, my family's story. Too soon I got to the end. . . .

. . . We learned about the melting pot. People came to America from all over the world to make a new life. When they got here, they met people from other countries, and pretty soon they

weren't English or German or Spanish or French anymore. They were just Americans. That happened with most people who came. It was different for some—for the Africans, who came as slaves, and for the Native Americans, who lived here first.

My ancestors were different, too. In the melting pot, they didn't melt. They kept their old ways and their language for more than two hundred years.

In some ways, my family history is like Sissy Norman's. My Anabaptists came from Germany at the same time her Huguenots came from France. They came for religious freedom.

But to me, my family seems more like Mimi Deng's. I'm the very first person in the Stoudt family to be raised as a regular American. My father and all the rest were raised to be Amish. If you visited them today in Lancaster, Pennsylvania, you'd think you were back in Germany in 1720.

They call themselves plain, but they don't mean plain like ugly. They mean simple or pure. They are very religious, and they stay away from things that are modern or fancy because it will take them away from their religion. They're

*strong people, and I'm proud my father taught
me their ways.*

Casey clapped when I finished. So did everybody else. When I got back to my seat, Sissy thanked me for putting in the stuff about her. She was so nice to me, I almost fainted.

Ms. Custer liked my report, too. On the way to lunch, she took me aside. "That report was A-plus work, Tyler. Ever think about becoming a writer, like your mother?"

"I will think about it," I agreed.

When I got to the cafeteria, Casey rushed up to me. "What took you so long?"

He yanked on my arm, dragged me to the table, and shoved me into a chair. Then he reached into his back pocket and tossed an envelope on the table in front of me. An envelope with a little window on it.

"Telegram. Delivered yesterday. I tried to call, but your dad said you were outside. I couldn't leave you a message, or he'd know something was up. Aren't you going to open it?"

My mouth felt so dry, my tongue got stuck. I could only nod. I picked up the envelope and read my name through the window. My name at Casey's address.

My fingers shook as I lifted the flap on the envelope and pulled out one thin page.

"What? What does it say? It's from your Massachusetts grandparents, isn't it?"

Mute, I stared at the paper. Stared at the seven printed words.

Tyler. I'm on my way. Margaret Tyler.

Chapter 25

Good things spread themselves out and make you wait a long time. Bad things clump together like they're ganging up. I should have told Papa about the Tyler letter. I knew it the minute I opened that telegram.

Somehow I made it through the afternoon, climbed on the bus, and rode the three miles to my house without passing out. I didn't dare pass out. I had to get home and warn Papa before Margaret Tyler arrived.

The bus dropped me at the end of our driveway, but there was dust in the air. And a strange car heading for our house.

I flew up the drive, breathing dust.

The car door opened, and a woman got out. I

couldn't see her face. She had silver hair, and she wore a suit and nice shoes. She looked exactly like a grandmother.

"Hello," I said, coming up behind her. I stopped to catch my breath.

She turned around slowly, like she was afraid. "Tyler? Are you Tyler?"

She had the kind of cold blue eyes that look right through you. "Yes, ma'am. I'm Tyler Stoudt."

The ice in her eyes melted then. It turned into tears and ran right down her face.

"You're a miracle, child," she said. She put her arms out, and I stepped into a hug.

She wasn't a big woman. She was about my size. It felt funny having her hug me. I was used to my tall father and his big bear hugs. I leaned on her shoulder, and she ruffled my hair with her fingers. Then she stepped back to look me over again.

"I'm your grandmother. Maggie Tyler. Your letter was the best thing that's happened to me in a very long time. I'd been traveling, and when I picked up the mail yesterday, I found your note. So I caught a noon flight to Cleveland. You got my telegram?"

"Yes. I got it."

"I hope I did the right thing, sending it to you at that other address. I would have called or written directly, but I was afraid your father might snatch you away again if he knew I was coming. Is Jakob at home?"

Her eyes froze up again, and I knew why. Papa had hidden me from her, and she was mad.

"I'll get him," I said. "Why don't you go in the house and sit down?"

If only I hadn't sent those dumb letters. They'd worked too well. If I knew Papa, he needed time, a week or two at least, to get over Levi's surprise visit. Now he had Grandmother Tyler sitting on the sofa in fancy clothes and high heels, waiting to yell at him.

I trudged over to the barn and pushed open the door. The smell of fresh-cut wood hit my nose. Papa was working the boards to help him think about Levi. Shoot, he'd need a whole tree's worth of boards when he found out about my grandmother. Maybe a whole forest.

He smiled as I walked into his shop. "I read your report, Tyler. You make a father proud."

"My report?"

"You leave it for me in the shop, no? A surprise? I have a surprise for you."

I had. The previous night, I'd made an extra

copy for him, and I'd sneaked it onto his work-bench early that morning. But that was nothing compared to the surprise that was waiting for him on the living room sofa.

"Papa . . . about that letter . . ."

"*Ja*. We talk it over already. I am glad you sent it. I have missed my family. And so to say thank you, I made this."

He reached under his bench and pulled out a package wrapped in brown paper.

My fingers fumbled as I opened it. Inside I found a tree, a tree carved out of cherry wood. The trunk of the tree said *The Stoudts*. He'd carved names into every branch. Three tiny wooden apples hung from the tree. One hung on my branch, one on Papa's, one on Uncle Levi's.

I took the little apple on my branch and wondered how Papa could make them so smooth and so round.

"Plenty of room on your tree," he told me. "When you grow up and have a family, I will make you more apples."

He reached out to hug me, but I backed away. If I didn't say the words soon, I'd never get them out.

"There's something else, Papa. There's . . .

there's another letter. I wrote two." I couldn't make my mouth say more.

Papa put one hand on each of my shoulders. He stared into my face without smiling. "Two letters?"

"Yes. One to your family. And one to Mama's." The words spilled out then. I'd held back too long. "I wanted to know about my family tree. Ms. Custer said to do my best. All the other kids knew where their ancestors came from. I felt funny not knowing. I'm sorry, Papa. I'm so sorry."

"So you wrote to the Tylers." He sighed. "The letter to Lancaster, that was a good thing. It brought Levi. This other letter, it makes me worry. Something bad can happen. They can come. But you're a good girl. You tell me, so I can be ready. You make a mistake, but you tell me."

He reached out to pat my hand, but I snatched it away. "No, Papa. I'm not good. I'm nosy and I cause trouble. And I didn't . . . I didn't tell you so you could be ready." I swallowed hard and took a deep breath. "I told you because she's here. Grandmother Tyler is here, and she wants to see you."

Papa's face flamed up. He didn't say a single word, just pushed past me toward the door.

I wanted to hide. I wanted to sit in the corner and play in the sawdust like I was little again. But I couldn't. I'd started this trouble. I had to be there for what happened next.

I heard their voices before I even got inside.

"You lied to us, Jakob. You told us the child died with Sarah."

"You are not welcome in this house, Margaret. You will leave."

"I will not leave before I get to know my grandchild. How could you do such a thing? A religious man! Honest! An upstanding Amish man! How could you lie about the child?"

"How could I tell the truth? *Ja,* I was an Amish man. Plain. Not rich or powerful. Would you and John Tyler let me keep my daughter? I just lost my wife; I could not lose the child, too."

I slipped inside and stood in the doorway. They could see me if they wanted to, but instead they glared at each other.

Grandmother's voice changed then. She sounded tired and old. "I lost my child, Jakob. Your wife was my only child. She was all I ever had. Surely you could have shared her baby with us."

Papa's voice got quiet, too, but I still heard anger in it. "You did not like me as husband for your daughter. You might not allow me as father to your grandchild. I could not take that chance."

"No judge would take a child away from her father unless he mistreated her, Jakob. And I . . . I didn't dislike you. . . . John . . . John was the one who wouldn't accept the marriage. I had to go along. But I still saw Sarah. I saw my daughter, and I knew she'd share my grandchild with me. When she died, I lost them both. And now John is gone, too. A stroke. Last summer."

"I'm sorry. For your loss of husband. And I didn't know about judges."

"What fools we were. We didn't even ask. We just assumed the baby was too premature to survive." My grandmother sniffed. "So many years. We lost so many years with the child. . . ."

I looked at them. The anger had blown out of them both, but neither one seemed to know what to do next. I slipped away to the kitchen and grabbed the cider jug. I poured three glasses and carried them to the living room.

They still didn't speak to each other.

I passed the cider, wishing it were a magic potion to make everything all right again.

The room stayed quiet.

I had to do something.

"Papa," I began. My voice shook, but I didn't let

that stop me. "Grandmother is right to be mad at you. I'm mad, too. Mad you hid me away."

I turned to look at Margaret Tyler. I took a deep breath.

"I'm mad at you, too, Grandmother. The Amish shunned Papa and Mama because of religion. You and my grandfather—you were worse. You didn't hurt them because of religion. It was just because . . . because Papa was different. And . . . and it's not fair. . . ."

They stared at me, and the room was so quiet I was sure they could hear my heart beating. Blood pounded loudly in my ears. Papa's eyes looked wet. Grandmother held her shoulders as stiff as an old oak tree.

Finally she spoke. "She's right, Jakob. The child is right. We are both at fault. Can we shake hands and start again? My life is empty. I could use a family."

Papa studied his hands, turning them over so he could see the backs and the fronts. I counted my heartbeats . . . ten, eleven, twelve . . .

Finally he nodded. "*Ja.* It is not good to be alone. I know it well. Tyler, these letters of yours brought a thunderstorm. But after a storm, the air is fresh. It blows clean again."

He reached out and shook my grandmother's

hand. Then somehow we were all hugging. Hugging and crying and smiling at the same time.

I took a deep breath. Papa was right. The air felt fresh and clean and full of hope. My family tree . . . it was alive again.

About the Author

Katherine Ayres has been a lover of books since childhood. Born in Columbus, Ohio, she began inventing stories before she could write them. Her love of literature continued through her first career as a teacher and elementary-school principal. She currently writes fiction for adults and for children.

Katherine Ayres lives with her husband and two daughters in Pittsburgh, where she skis, golfs, gardens, quilts, and rebuilds old houses between writing sessions. She has published stories in *Cricket, Spider, Ladybug,* and other magazines. *Family Tree* is her first novel.